Praise for
Rachelle J. Christensen's
Award-winning Novels

Hawaiian Masquerade is the perfect summer read. Set on the beautiful island of Kauai, you will fall in love with the characters, the story line, the setting, and most of all the romance. I would highly recommend this fast-paced, fabulous clean romance.

--Cami Checketts, author of *The Feisty One: A Billionaire Bride Pact Romance*

Christensen has done a magnificent job of putting together an unlikely match and letting it challenge the characters to grow, change, and become better together than they were apart. This is a wonderful, sweet romance that you'll want to stay up to finish.

-Lucy McConnell, author of the *Billionaire Marriage Brokers* series

How to Fetch a Fiancé

Other Works by Rachelle

Diamond Rings Are Deadly Things (Wedding Planner Mysteries #1)

Veils and Vengeance (#2)

Proposals and Poison (#3)

The Soldier's Bride (A Music Box Romance #1)

Carve Me a Melody (A Music Box Romance #2)

Hawaiian Masquerade (Burke Billionaire Romance #1)

The Billionaire's Stray Heart (Burke Billionaire Romance #2)

River Whispers

Wrong Number

Caller ID

Novellas:

Silver Cascade Secrets

Double Take

Hope for Christmas: An Echo Ridge Romance

The Kiss Thief: An Echo Ridge Romance

The Princess Bride of Riodan: An Echo Ridge Romance

Coming Home to Love: An Echo Ridge Romance

Nonfiction:

What Every 6th Grader Needs to Know: 10
Secrets to Connect Moms & Daughters

Lost Children: Coping with Miscarriage

Ultimate Life: Create a Life Worth Living in 9 Simple Steps

How to Fetch a Fiancé

Rachelle J. Christensen

Thrills for the Heart

FOR A LIMITED TIME

Sign up for Rachelle's
VIP Mailing List
to get your *FREE* book.

Get started here:
www.rachellechristensen.com

Dedication

To everyone who has loved a dog and learned something about how to love others in the process. And to the real Duke, a German Shepherd service dog for my neighbor, a Vietnam War veteran. He will always be remembered.

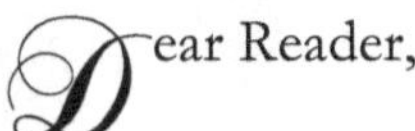ear Reader,

Every once in a while an opportunity comes up that must not be set aside, put off, ignored, or passed. The moment must be recognized—immediately—and acted upon with haste. The chance to cross the Must Love Dog series with the Destination Billionaire Romance series and have the amazing, bestselling author Rachelle J. Christensen write *How to Fetch a Fiancé* was a divergence in the path that demanded exploration.

The results are astounding!

Rachelle J. Christensen has a gift for painting life into her stories. She not only understands the art of writing, she picks up the brush and gets to work creating realistic images and life-like characters. This is the perfect story to disappear into for hours.

You may find a bit of yourself in these pages; or, you may find a best friend. One thing's for sure, you'll find sweet romance and a great read.

Happy Reading,
Lucy McConnell
Author of the Billionaire Marriage Brokers series

Chapter 1

"Fetch!" Audrey called as she threw the Frisbee across the park. Her German Shepherd, Duke, launched after it with a yip. He careened through a copse of trees, making Audrey cringe, but showed up a moment later with the yellow Frisbee in his mouth. She reached for it and Duke pulled back. "Hand it over," Audrey said in her best motherly tone. Duke let go of the Frisbee, his tongue lolling to the side. "Yes! Good boy!" She patted him on the head, happy with his progress. "Keep up these manners, and you'll be ready to play fetch with the girls."

Duke straightened up and looked past her to where Katie and Lizzie, ages nine and six, were swinging and giggling. Audrey watched the girls with a smile. They had adjusted well to Tennessee, although the move had been full of drastic changes: no more Daddy, all new friends, and even a huge climate change from Oregon. It had been almost two years now, and Audrey's stomach still clenched when she thought very long on the life she had before her husband cheated on her. She shook her head and turned back to Duke. "Ready?"

Duke stood at attention, determination in his eyes. Audrey flipped her wrist, sending the bright yellow Frisbee on a somewhat wobbly course through the sky. "Fetch!"

An invisible gust of wind pushed the Frisbee off course, and it veered right toward the sidewalk. Audrey watched in horror as a man in a suit, talking on a cell phone, walked toward the flying disc. Before she could call out a warning, the Frisbee hit him in the side of the head, and Duke barreled into him, chasing after his toy. "Duke, no!"

The man fell on the grass, his cell phone flying behind him. Audrey sprinted toward the man, arriving just as Duke dropped the Frisbee and licked his face. "No, Duke. Off!" Audrey waved him away and crouched over the man lying on his back, his eyes closed. Surely the Frisbee hadn't knocked him out, had it? A red welt rose up on his temple, and Audrey parted his thick brown hair to assess the wound. "That's going to be tender. I'm so sorry."

He grabbed her wrist, wincing. "It already is."

"Oh! You're alive—I mean, conscious?" She put her hand on his chest, surprised at the hard physique that was well covered by his pinstriped suit. Duke hovered next to her, and she elbowed him away to keep her dog from licking the poor man again.

The man chuckled, and then he looked up at her with eyes so brown they were almost black. He touched the side of his head again, his dark eyebrows pulling together. "Stunned, embarrassed, *and* still alive." He sat up, wincing once more.

"I'm so sorry," Audrey said. "The wind came out of nowhere and launched the Frisbee into your head."

The man looked around and held a hand out in the perfectly still air. "What wind?"

Audrey straightened, noticing that there wasn't even a breath of movement. She closed her eyes. Not only had she hit this guy in the head with a Frisbee, now he probably thought she was making up things to excuse her abysmal throwing skills. She shrugged. "It was there. I'll admit I'm not a great aim, since I'm throwing for my dog anyway, but I saw it. Duke was headed one way and the Frisbee veered off—right into the side of your head."

"Well, I'm all right now." The man rolled his shoulders back and stood slowly. Audrey couldn't be sure, but it looked like he was biting the inside of his cheek. He looked at Duke, and his jaw started ticking.

"Please don't blame my dog. Duke has a lot of spirit, but I work with him every day."

He shook his head. "I don't." He turned and scanned the grass until he found his phone. He bent down and picked it up, examining it before sliding it into his suit pocket.

Audrey blew out a breath, relieved that she hadn't caused his phone to break. "Well, again, I'm really sorry."

"Apology accepted. Better work on that aim, though." He winked.

"Hey, I can't control the wind," Audrey protested.

He looked up toward the sky. "I believe you. I'm just wondering what message God was trying to send me with that Frisbee."

Audrey pulled her shoulders back, the familiar tense knot popping out between her shoulder blades. Her ex-husband, Drew, was an upstanding member of their congregation while he was cheating with the preacher's wife. "God doesn't have anything to do with it. It was an accident. That's all."

The man pulled his gaze from the heavens and back to her face. "I think the man upstairs has a lot more to do with things than we ever give him credit for."

The well of emotions Audrey kept tamped down started simmering beneath her skin. "I'm glad you think so. I need to go check on my girls. If you'll excuse me."

"Okay." He nodded, but continued staring at her. "Have a good day."

"C'mon, Duke." Audrey grabbed the Frisbee and walked as fast as she could toward the swing set. She hadn't found a reason to give the man upstairs credit for anything in the past two years except ruining her life. She could still feel the guy she'd hit staring at her as she approached her girls, but she didn't look back. There was no room in her life for good-looking men who still smiled after being hit in the head by a Frisbee.

Troy Jackson stood on the sidewalk for a few seconds more, watching the petite red-haired lady practically sprint toward the swing set with her German Shepherd chasing after her. Those red curls looked burnished in the sunlight, and even though she wasn't facing him, he could still see her clear blue eyes. She'd narrowed them, her expression filled with hurt, just before she'd left.

When she'd touched his head, he'd felt something. He'd been closed off for so long that it was barely recognizable, but the power coming from her couldn't be ignored. And then her eyes … She'd left in such a hurry, running from her feelings so fast that he didn't even get her name.

Troy smiled. When the woman had started talking about the wind knocking the Frisbee into his head, he couldn't believe it. Just moments before, he had been on the phone with a businessman wanting him to take on a new client. As owner and CEO of Arise Music, a Christian record company, Troy had to be very selective with the singers he brought in. Every day he prayed and asked God to help him run his business the best way possible. He'd been on the fence about this new singer and was worrying how to make the decision before the Frisbee had hit him, ending the call and helping him make the choice that he had been ignoring all along.

He was about to explain himself to the red-haired woman, but as soon as he started talking about God, the woman had turned stiff and cold and left. Troy was hoping to introduce himself before he inadvertently ended the conversation. He kept thinking about the redhead all the way back to his office on Music Row. The little bungalow where he worked still seemed like a dream come true sometimes. His father had asked him a few months ago, "Why haven't you converted to a high-rise building with all the dollars you have hanging around? Why not go to a nice new office space?"

But Troy loved his office, and he liked staying close to the roots of the business. His company was approachable, and he liked that because he never knew who God would send through his door next. When he reached his office, Mike Cheatham, the A&R director of Arise, was waiting for him as if he'd scheduled an appointment, which, as usual, he hadn't. Troy hardly had a chance to say hello before Mike launched in on the next task on his agenda.

"Troy, it's past time for making decisions on the new vocal coach for Felicia Perry. Can we please take a chance on this woman I've been researching? She's new to the scene here in Nashville, but I think she can offer something that others we've interviewed haven't so far."

Troy stuck his hands in his pockets and smiled. Mike often put in more hours than Troy, so he did his best to work with Mike's requests, but he'd already gone over this twice. "It's been a rough day, Mike. I just got knocked in the head by a Frisbee trying to walk through the park. I'm wondering what I'm missing here. I told you I don't want to try someone who is untested on a new talent."

Mike paced back and forth across the office. He was in his mid-forties, bald, and had a slight paunch to his belly. He had jowls bordering on bulldog, and that image always stayed in Troy's mind. Mike was a bulldog when it came to the business, and he was good at his job. He turned to face Troy. "Just give her one shot. I can bring her in to work with Felicia so we can see what we think."

As the arts and repertoire director, or A&R director, Mike was assigned to work with every artist at Arise to fine-tune the artist's abilities; that included working with naïve young singers untested on the stage as well as prima donnas (and yes, some men fit that description, too). Felicia was not a prima donna. She was an innocent young girl from Alabama who had grown up on Bible songs and wanted to be part of a Christian band. "You know I don't like messing with these things too much," Troy said. "Felicia's voice is beautiful, crystal clear, and she has a message. We need to help her with some of those wild pitch points, but I don't want somebody telling her she has to have all this soulful stuff to be a Christian singer."

Mike was already nodding. "I know that. I wouldn't approach you with this idea if I wasn't sure that she could do it."

Troy turned and looked out the large picture window of his office. Late May was a beautiful time in Nashville, with mild temperatures and everything looking green and vibrant. Part of him wished he could head out early and go for a drive. Instead, he closed his eyes for a moment and thought about what needed to happen. The right vocal coach had to have special talents to refine the singer's voice, while at the same time not changing it into something that it wasn't.

"Troy, it's a one-time session to see if we like her. Come on." Mike's deep voice had a bit of growl to it.

Troy sighed. He'd hired Mike because he trusted him, and Mike hadn't let him down yet. It was time to put that trust into action again. "Okay, go in and get it scheduled with Rachel. And I'll at least listen."

Mike clapped Troy on the back. "Hey, maybe God was knocking sense into you with that Frisbee." He laughed as he left the office.

Troy sat down at his desk and put his hand to his temple— it was tender to the touch. He immediately thought of the woman from the park. He could still see her red hair catching the sunlight as she walked away. He didn't know what it meant, but hopefully with patience he would find out.

Chapter 2

udrey Blair did not get along with church, heaven, or prayers. None of those things had given her any help or warning when her scumbag of a husband Drew had cheated on her two years ago. In spite of the turn her life had taken, Audrey had divorced Drew and moved to Nashville, Tennessee, to start up her vocal coaching business. While living in Oregon, she'd built an online business using video tutorials to coach people in the art of singing, transporting melody and story through beautiful clear vocal pitches. Audrey loved her work, but when her marriage fell apart and Drew decided he didn't want anything to do with his daughters, she determined to stop the cycle of hurt. She took a chance and moved to Nashville, far away from Drew's influence and to the center of all good music. She'd been a country-western music fan for most of her life, and up until recently an ardent fan and follower of Christian rock. The songs that she rocked her baby to soothed and comforted her back then, until God had seemingly turned his back on her, and Audrey switched off the music for a while. It wasn't until she moved back to Nashville that she started listening to Christian music again, telling herself that she needed to inundate herself with all varieties of music so she could analyze those voices and be prepared to be a vocal coach for one of the most successful singers in the world. At least that was her dream—the one she'd been working on for the past decade.

She smoothed down her dark green business suit and tucked a strand of hair behind her ear. Today one of her biggest breaks was about to happen, she could sense it. She'd experienced bad luck last week when she hit that man with a Frisbee, so today had to be better, right? She didn't let the doubts creep into her mind; she concentrated on success. She was going to Arise Music Studios to meet with Mike Cheatham and an up-and-coming singer, Felicia Perry. Audrey had listened to Felicia's demo songs and could hear that the young woman had talent. With a little coaching, she might be the next big hit on the radio stations. Audrey took in a deep breath and let it out slowly through her nose. She felt her diaphragm fill up with air and then pushed it slowly out, counting to ten. She loved singing, but teaching was in her blood.

"Katie, Lizzie," Audrey called. "Let's go. We have just enough time to go through the drive-through for an ice cream if you hurry."

"I want chocolate!" Lizzie squealed. The six-year-old danced around in a circle, chanting, "Chocolate, chocolate, chocolate!"

Katie folded her arms and rolled her eyes. "I'll take a twist."

Audrey smiled. This new grown-up phase that Katie was going through was cute, although at times a bit tiring. She didn't want her girls to grow up too fast. She wanted to love on them and cuddle with them for as long as she could.

Duke yipped from the washroom, his signal that he didn't want to be left out of all the fun.

"I know, Duke," Audrey crooned, "but you can't come with us today."

Duke's left ear twitched, the way it always did when he was disappointed. Some people might think she was silly, but Audrey knew Duke had real feelings, the same way that her dog intuitively picked up on her feelings. There had been countless times over the past two years when Duke had comforted her as she worked through the hostile emotions and painful memories related to her ex-husband. Shortly after her divorce, Audrey had rescued Duke, a stray dog from the local animal shelter. Duke was just a puppy and he'd filled a place in Audrey's broken heart immediately.

Audrey rubbed behind his ears, and he pushed his head against her hand. "Later tonight, we'll go for a walk. Hopefully to celebrate."

Duke whined.

"Now you be a good boy and go on out to the backyard and play." She patted his head again and clicked her tongue. Duke turned and obediently exited the washroom through his large dog door, the black tip of his tail wagging.

Audrey took the girls to the drive-through and deposited them at her best friend's home a few minutes later, their ice cream cones almost finished. LuAnne Clark met her at the door. Her black hair fell in short waves around her head, and her boatneck shirt in a bright yellow was beautiful against her dark skin. LuAnne pointed at Audrey's shirt, and her Southern accent softened each word. "Well, if looks were all it took to get the job, you'd have it. I told you that color green would look great on you."

"You were right, as usual." Audrey put her hand on Lizzie's back. "Now be good for Lu, and don't be arguing with Davon and Whitney." LuAnne's kids were eight and six, perfect playmates and sometimes troublemakers when paired with Audrey's girls.

"We will, Mom," Katie said.

"Thanks so much for doing this for me, Lu," Audrey said.

"Hey, it helps me out. Keeps the kids busy." LuAnne guided the kids through the door. "Good luck. Call me as soon as you know any details."

Audrey waved as she drove away. The traffic on the way into Nashville was always a little bit snarly, but she loved living in Franklin, a suburb of Nashville only thirty minutes out of the big city. The town was beautifully kept and manicured. It was a stretch, but Audrey had moved into Echo Estates on the fumes of her dreams and hefty child support and alimony that Drew had to cover each month. She still questioned her decisions at times, but she was determined to take the steps needed to support her family in case the money ever dropped off with Drew. She certainly couldn't trust him with their marriage, so why would she trust him to take care of his children? Audrey gave her head a little shake. She wasn't going to think about Drew for the rest of the day. Today was the day for conquering dreams.

She made it into Nashville with time to spare, found a parking space behind Arise Music Studios, and hesitated as she stepped onto the sidewalk. She was on Music Row, the place where dreams were crushed or fulfilled in the music business. She opened the door and saw a pert little secretary with blonde bombshell hair and other things that reminded her of Dolly Parton. The girl smiled broadly.

"Howdy-do. How can I help you?" Her Southern drawl was cute and definitely more Southern than Tennessee.

"I'm Audrey Blair. I'm here to meet with Mike Cheatham." She began twisting her hand and stopped, clutching the edges of her skirt

"Oh, it's you!" She extended her hand. "I'm Rachel Graham, Mr. Jackson's secretary. "I'm rooting for you. Felicia is a darling girl, but she needs a little refinin'." She leaned over her computer, and her blonde hair moved, but only slightly. Rachel typed something on her keyboard and then stood. "Right this way."

"Thank you," Audrey replied. "And thank you for the well-wishes. I need all the help I can get."

"Here you are. Mike and Troy are waiting for you. They'll talk to you about Felicia before you meet with her." The blonde sauntered away down the hall.

Audrey stepped into the room and came face to face with the very man she'd almost knocked out with the Frisbee last week. She closed her eyes for two seconds and opened them, but he was still standing there, a funny lopsided smile on his ruggedly handsome face. Audrey felt the heat rising to her cheeks. "Hi, I'm Audrey Blair, also known as the Ultimate Frisbee activist."

The man burst out laughing. He walked toward her with hand outstretched. "Troy Jackson, owner and CEO of Arise Music."

"Wait a minute. You two have met?" Mike asked.

Audrey shook her head. She opened her mouth to speak, but Troy answered first.

"She's the one who knocked me in the head with the Frisbee. Helped me from making a pretty bad mistake." He turned to her and winked. "I really need to thank you for that." He touched the side of his temple, where a faint pink line still stood out against his dark hair.

Audrey wasn't sure how to respond. When she'd left the conversation, it had been borderline rude and definitely letting too much of her past show. "I had no idea who you were. If I did, I would've tried not to hit you with the Frisbee in the first place."

Mike and Troy both chuckled. "Well, you're here now. Let's talk shop."

Troy motioned for her to sit in a chair next to his beautiful black walnut desk. Mike sat next to her. "So let's start by having you tell Troy a little bit of what you told me, your vision for Felicia Perry and what you can do for her."

Audrey swallowed. All she could hear was her own voice ringing in her ears, claiming that God had nothing to do with anything. She had told that to the owner of Arise Music. The owner, Troy Jackson, who now sat in front of her and didn't seem to be holding any judgment for what she'd said. There had been a curious look in his eyes; he was probably wondering what would make someone say something so bold and brash.

Audrey refocused on the topic at hand. "Felicia is a gifted vocalist. With training and refinement, her voice will be a clear ensign to the world of her message of truth." Audrey cringed inwardly, knowing that her words were in direct contrast to the flippant statement she'd given to Troy last week. She let her chin dip down and continued forward. "The key is not to lose the unique quality of her voice in the refinement. A lot of vocal coaches utilize techniques that take away bits of individuality from the singer's voice."

Troy leaned forward. "I'd like to see more of what you're talking about. As you know, we scheduled Felicia to be here in ten minutes. Mike and I will observe you in training with her. Let's see how it goes." Troy stood. "Now, my favorite part. Let me take you back to the recording studio."

Mike stood as well and followed Audrey and Troy out into the hall. They walked down a short hallway to the next door, which opened into a recording studio with all the latest state-of-the-art equipment. Three computers sat along the dash overlooking a sound quality room with several microphones. Audrey had been in rooms like this before, but she could tell that a lot of care had gone into putting this room together and keeping it in pristine condition. Everything was separated from the actual recording portion of the room. She followed Troy as he showed her their new digital audio workstation; the studio monitors were larger than she was used to and with a glance, Audrey noticed that everything Arise Music used was top of the line.

"I'd like to try something first," Audrey said.

"What's that?" Mike asked.

"I'd like to take the pop filter off the mic." Audrey stepped into the recording room. She walked up to one of the microphones and carefully unscrewed the arm holding the thin fabric screen in front of the microphone. "Let Felicia sing and then listen to herself. Then I'll put the pop filter back on and let her sing and listen again."

Mike nodded. "I'm sure that'll be fine." He spoke through the sound system, and Audrey was impressed by the quality of the sound in the room.

"It's little things like that," Audrey said as she returned to the line of screens next to Troy and Mike. "Things that make the singers more aware of their own instrument that I like to concentrate on at first."

Troy nodded. "Have at it. You look like you know your way around a recording studio."

"I do. It's one of my favorite places, although I've never been in one this nice."

"So you've done some recording yourself?" Troy asked.

"Mostly backup vocals. I'm a singer-songwriter first, but I found my true passion in teaching later on." Audrey ran her finger along the edge of the desk. "It's nice to have the experience from both sides for teaching."

"I agree," Troy said.

"Looks like she's here." Mike motioned toward the door.

A young woman, barely twenty-one years old, walked into the room. Her long blonde hair was braided to the side, and she wore deep red lipstick. Audrey was worried she might be a prima donna, but then she noticed the way Felicia's fingers twitched, and how her throat tightened as she smiled. This girl probably threw up just before she went onstage every time.

Mike motioned toward Audrey. "Felicia, this is Audrey Blair. She's a talented vocal coach with lots of innovative ideas for training new singers for the stage. We'd like to see how you two work together today."

Felicia nodded and held out her hand. "Pleased to meet you."

Audrey shook her hand, firmly. "I listened to your demos, and I'm impressed with your talent. Thank you for taking the time to work with me today." Audrey smiled and looked directly into Felicia's light green eyes.

Felicia returned the smile. "I know I need to work on things. I love singing. I'll do anything to make my voice last so that I can sing when I'm a hundred years old."

"I like that attitude," Audrey replied. "Let's get to work, shall we?"

For the next forty-five minutes, Audrey worked with Felicia, beginning with a dozen different vocal drills and then recording Felicia singing Bible hymns from her childhood. They listened to the recordings, and Audrey analyzed everything. Felicia was a willing student, and Audrey could see within a few minutes that she was telling the truth when she said she wanted to sing until she was one hundred years old. Every time Felicia started singing, Audrey made notes, and it was usually by about the fifth note that she'd hit her zone. The quality of her voice was undeniably passionate about the message that she was singing. Audrey had Felicia lie down on the ground with a stack of books on her stomach and sing "Amazing Grace." The exercises were to help her be more in tune with her diaphragm and the strength of her stomach muscles while moving oxygen in and out of her lungs. Even though Felicia had books stacked on top of her, the old favorite brought tears to Audrey's eyes. She blinked rapidly and pretended to write extra notes until the moisture cleared.

The anger burning inside her chest helped those feelings vanish most of the time. As long as she stayed angry with God, and angry at all that He had let happen to her perfectly planned life, she didn't need to feel. But at times, even the anger wasn't enough to mask the memories of God's love and how it used to touch her heart.

At the end of the session, Audrey was encouraged and hopeful. If Troy and Mike could see even a glimmer of her ability in coaching Felicia and what they'd done in such a short time, they would surely hire her. Her throat clenched as they met back in Troy's office.

"Felicia, that was impressive to watch." Troy grinned broadly at Felicia, and then at Audrey. "Mike and I made our decision. Have you made yours?"

Felicia nodded quickly. "Yes? Heavens yes, please let me work with Audrey." She leaned over and gripped Audrey's hand.

Stunned, Audrey turned to Felicia and then her gaze moved to Mike and Troy. "You mean …?"

"You're hired, if you'd like the job," Troy replied.

"Yes, I'd be honored to work with Felicia and you." Audrey's heart pounded. It was really happening. She was sitting in front of a man worth over a billion dollars, and he was telling her she was hired.

"I'd like to talk to you and get things scheduled out. Let's have you working with Felicia every day for two or three hours. Does that sound all right?" Troy stood and handed Audrey a folder. "Here are the employee forms. If you'll fill these out before you leave today ..."

"And Audrey," Mike said, "we'd like you to consider working with a few other clients on our list as well."

If Audrey's heart was thumping hard before, she didn't know how to describe what it was doing now. "You would? I mean, that sounds wonderful."

"Good, we'll get you all set up with Rachel," Mike said.

Everyone stood and exited the office. Troy put his hand on her back, and his touch sent a spark through her middle. "I look forward to working with you," he said with a smile.

Audrey didn't dare call LuAnne, because she would only scream in her ear. Instead, she grinned all the way through Nashville traffic as she drove back out to Franklin and parked in front of her neighbor's house. She hopped out, still smiling, hardly believing what had just happened. She had a job. Not only a job, but she was working with one of the biggest Christian record companies in Nashville.

She knocked on the door twice, bouncing up and down on her toes as she waited for Lu to answer. As soon as her friend opened the door, Audrey squealed, "I got the job!"

"Congratulations!" LuAnne cried, pulling Audrey into a hug. "I knew you could do it."

Hearing the commotion, the kids scampered around the corner. Audrey beamed at her two daughters. "Guess what? Mommy is going to work with a new singer now."

Katie's gaze darted from LuAnne back to her mother. "Does that mean you'll be gone a lot?"

Audrey sensed the worry in her little girl's eyes. "Just the same as usual." Ever since they moved to Nashville, she had gone to clients' homes to teach voice lessons and to give vocal coaching. The girls were used to her working part time each week, and she was grateful that for now, things would stay the same. LuAnne had already agreed to continue watching the girls during the summer.

"Yeah, Mommy is the best!" Lizzie cried.

Audrey leaned over and hugged her two girls. "Thank you. This means a lot to Mommy."

"So what do you think of the new singer you'll be working with?" LuAnne asked.

Audrey stood and turned to her friend. The kids ran off as soon as they saw that their moms were engaged in conversation, allowing a few more minutes to play. "She's young, inexperienced, but I love her attitude. I think it's going to work out great."

"I have a pitcher of iced tea. Care for some?" LuAnne inclined her head toward the kitchen, and Audrey nodded. LuAnne's ebony curls still looked as sophisticated as they had that morning, and her bright smile mirrored Audrey's grin. LuAnne was one of the most driven women Audrey knew, but in her home, she always seemed at peace. She followed her friend into the kitchen and sat on one of the five matching barstools at the counter. LuAnne was the assistant principal at the private school their kids attended together. She was one of the first friends Audrey had made within a week of moving to Nashville.

"I'm happy for you, Audrey." LuAnne sipped her iced tea.

"Thank you," Audrey replied. "It feels like the right thing to do. I've been working for this kind of break for years. I keep pinching myself, wondering if it's really true."

"You're going to do great. And what's more, your work will make that girl's dreams come true."

"I hope so. I was a little worried when I first arrived at the meeting, especially when I discovered that the owner of the record company is the same man I hit in the head with the Frisbee last week."

LuAnne's mouth dropped open. "Not really?"

Audrey nodded. "Really."

LuAnne leaned forward. "And he still hired you?"

Audrey hadn't told LuAnne all the details of the Frisbee incident, and she didn't plan to. "He's a pretty good-natured guy."

"Single and handsome too?" LuAnne chuckled.

Audrey shrugged. "He is, but I'm not worried about that. The job is my focus."

"Hmm, well, you keep telling yourself that now, and I think you'll do just fine in this new job."

Audrey nodded her agreement, checking her thoughts that were wandering to that moment in the park when she'd touched the side of Troy's head, her hand on his chest with his heart beating steadily beneath it. His dark brown eyes were warm and inviting, and earlier today she'd caught him staring at her intently a few times. She liked the way his dark hair fell across his forehead. He was a good-looking guy, and she could admit that much and keep him at arm's length. Hopefully.

Chapter 3

Troy sat in his black leather office chair and looked out toward the window at the busy street on Music Row. The heart of Nashville was pumping this time of day, and sometimes Troy felt like he could almost hear the music in the pulse of the city. Things were looking good at Arise Music. The last two sessions he'd observed with Audrey and Felicia were impressive. Audrey had fire and grit, and she was willing to infuse her determination and enthusiasm into Felicia's budding talent. He'd seen a different side of Felicia the past week as she worked with Audrey. Under her tutelage, the singer was bursting from a shell that he hadn't known was there, her wings unfolding and allowing the world to see the intricate patterns on those wings.

The music business was often risky and a somewhat unstable path. When you added in the Christian element to the music, it became even more difficult. Troy worked hard every day to meet the needs of his listeners and help them to be uplifted by the music he produced. At the same time, he was working with artists who were creating music for the same purposes. It was important in his business for the musicians to lead a life walking in the path that God had laid before them. Someone like Felicia Perry, barely twenty-one years old, was a prime candidate for temptation, worldliness, and a runaway life of too much fame and fortune. He'd seen it happen before, always with regret. Maybe he felt it more than most because of his own past mistakes. But he had turned his life around and invested everything he had into building up Christian radio. He still remembered one of his lowest points; it had been a Christian pop song that had pierced through the clouds of darkness to his soul.

His computer pinged with a message from his secretary, Rachel.

Can you meet with Audrey for a few minutes?

Troy looked at her name on the screen. It was still hard to believe that the redhead from the park now worked at Arise. **Sure, let's meet in ten minutes.**

When he received the confirmation for the impromptu appointment, Troy tried to ignore the increase in his heart rate. For some reason, he was anxious to see her, and it shouldn't be because she was beautiful and interesting, but Troy had trouble focusing on his work for the next ten minutes.

Audrey came to his office eleven minutes later. "Thanks for letting me pop in. I promise not to take too much of your time." She stood in the doorway uncertainly.

"Please have a seat." Troy stood and motioned for her to sit in one of the two wingback chairs facing his desk. "How can I help you today?"

"Well, things are going really great with Felicia. I'm encouraged by the progress that she's making in such a short time. She's a sweet young woman." Audrey twisted her hands together in her lap.

"But?" Troy tilted his head, studying Audrey carefully.

"I didn't say 'but.'"

"I know … but," Troy chuckled, "it does seem like you have more to say. Whatever it is, don't be worried. I want to make this work as much as you do."

Audrey looked up, her blue eyes striking against her creamy skin. "Well, Felicia has asked me to help her with another song that she's writing. We hadn't gone over the specifics as to how much you'd like me to work with her. I don't want to step on any toes."

Troy smiled. "Whatever you feel she needs that Felicia is willing to work on, we're happy to arrange it."

Audrey nodded. "Thank you."

Troy waited for her to say more, but she started twisting her hands again, so he decided to keep the conversation going. "I know it's only been a couple weeks, but do you enjoy working here?"

Audrey brightened. "I do. The environment here's wonderful. I always dreamed about working on Music Row. I bet you love that view." Audrey pointed to the large picture window next to his desk.

The street was lined with trees, bursting with every shade of green imaginable. The trees stood as sentinels to dozens of record companies—many housed in small bungalows like Troy's. The street held a constant stream of traffic and pedestrians, a mix of tourists and locals, and the music. It was everywhere, in the hopeful steps of the young artist who had just dropped off his demo record to the company across the street, or the older couple walking along, their hands swinging to an unseen beat.

Troy nodded. "I do. Some people say I should build a high-rise down the street, join some of the bigger companies, but I like it here."

"I like that you're approachable," Audrey said.

"I like that you get that. It's how I want to be. I hold on to that idea every time my dad pesters me about investing more of my money into a newer building."

Audrey's cheeks flushed. "How many singers do you work with?" She'd done some research, but the internet wasn't always one hundred percent reliable.

"We're sitting right at thirty-eight now." Troy tapped his finger on the large planning calendar spread across his desk. "I have a team that keeps track of everything, of course, but I like to keep tabs on the heart of my business. Some of our musicians are busier than others, producing more than others. But all in all, we keep things pretty busy around here."

"Well, I'm glad to be part of it." She shifted as if she was about to stand up.

"Is there something else you wanted to talk to me about?" Troy pushed as lightly as he could.

Audrey's shoulders rolled inward. "That day in the park, it's been bothering me ever since. I wish I hadn't said those things to you."

Immediately, Troy recalled how Audrey's face turned hard when he mentioned God. There was a story behind her beautiful blue eyes, and heaven help him, but he wanted to know what it was. He stood and walked around the side of his desk, taking a seat next to her. "I don't hold any judgment. We all have days like those."

Audrey bit her bottom lip and nodded. "Thank you for understanding."

Troy shrugged. "We all have stories—some good, some bad. Maybe you'll have to tell me more of your story sometime."

"Maybe." Audrey's lips twitched, as if she were choosing her words carefully. "You've probably heard stories like mine before—nothing new."

"My door is always open." He leaned forward, and bumped her knee with his own. "Even if you think the story isn't worth telling, I'd still like to hear it."

Audrey watched him, her blue eyes pulling him in. He smiled, wishing there was some other reason that he could keep talking to her. Then he snapped his fingers. "I almost forgot. Our company picnic is coming up in two weeks, on a Monday night. You and your family are invited."

"Really? That would be wonderful."

"Yes, Rachel can give you all the details, but I'll tell you that we'll have some special musical appearances for sure, and there will be lots of fun activities for the kids. One of my favorite events is the cupcake walk. I head that up every year." Troy tried to stop himself from rambling, but he wanted Audrey to come. He wondered if there would be a chance for more casual conversation at the party.

"Thank you," Audrey said. "My girls will be over the moon. They love music."

"And will you be bringing a plus-one?" He gathered from Audrey's documents that she was divorced, but he wasn't sure if she was involved in another relationship.

Audrey shook her head. "No, just me and my two girls. Unless you'd like me to bring Duke along."

Troy laughed and relief flooded his chest; at the same time, he tried to reprimand himself for his interest in Audrey. "I think Duke and I need another chance to be introduced properly. Last time was a little rough."

Now it was Audrey's turn to laugh. "He's come a long way, but he still struggles with his manners."

"Well, he did a good job of rescuing me." Troy rubbed the side of his head, thinking of the incident with the Frisbee.

"I'm glad you think so. We've had him for two years now—he was a stray dog someone dropped off at the animal shelter. I took him to dog obedience classes last year. He is very smart, as most German Shepherds are, but Duke seems to read my mind sometimes."

Troy was secretly glad that he'd had the run-in with Audrey, because it gave them a connection outside the office. "I had a German Shepherd. She was scared to death of thunder, but she was the best protector of our family."

Audrey chuckled. "Duke gets overprotective when Katie and Lizzie get in a fight. It sure helps me out since they don't have a dad around." Her eyes widened, as if realizing she'd said too much.

He wasn't sure if it was the memories of his past or the possibilities of the future that made him nervous every time he caught himself staring at Audrey Blair too long. The woman was barely over five feet, and her striking blue eyes were windows to her soul even though she kept herself carefully closed off. Troy wanted to learn more about her, but he also didn't want to cross the line. "I'm glad you have Duke around. Those girls are lucky to have him too."

"We're all lucky to have him." Audrey scooted off her chair. "Well, I'd better be going. Thanks again for taking a few minutes to talk with me," Audrey said. "I really appreciate this opportunity."

"I'm glad you feel that way, because I feel the same." He saw Audrey out the door and returned to his desk, but he didn't sit down. Troy had a new contract to go over, and he needed his full concentration for the task, but the room was charged with Audrey's presence, and he wanted to soak it up before it faded away. It had been years since he'd felt even a sliver of interest in a woman. Could it finally be time for him to find love?

Chapter 4

Near the end of her second week of work at Arise Music, Audrey stayed a little later than she had planned after her session with Felicia to write notes for the next session. When she walked out to her car, she opened the door and stood there for a minute, feeling the heat emanating from the interior. Then she got inside and turned the key, but all she heard was a clicking sound. Audrey groaned as she continued to turn the key and no engine started, no air conditioning turned on to save her from the heat. She popped the hood of her car and looked inside, but she didn't really know much about cars.

Beyond checking the coolant level and keeping her windshield wiper fluid full, she wasn't really qualified to do much else. She pulled out her cell phone so she could call LuAnne, who was watching her girls again, and then a tow truck.

"Hey, are you having some trouble?" Troy asked as he walked around the side of the building.

Audrey sighed. "Yes. I know it isn't the battery, because I just replaced it a few months ago."

"Let me take a look," Troy said. He sat in her car, adjusted the seat back for his long legs, and tried starting it, getting the same clicking noise she had. Then he hopped out and looked under the hood for a few minutes, and frowned. "I think it could be your alternator."

Audrey pursed her lips together. She didn't want to break down in front of her boss, no matter how much she hated car trouble. She took a deep breath and let it out slowly. "I guess I'll call a tow truck. Do you know any good mechanics around this area?"

"I do. Wait on calling that tow truck. My mechanic has a towing service. Why don't you let me give him a call for you?" Troy shut the hood of her car. "He's honest and great to work with. I bet he could have your car fixed by tomorrow evening."

Audrey found herself nodding. "That would be wonderful, thanks." She waited while Troy made the call, listening to his end of the conversation.

When he was finished, Troy smiled. "He'll be right over to get it. In the meantime, you'll need a way home."

"Yes, I was just trying to figure that out because my best friend is watching my kids."

"You live in Franklin, right?" Troy asked.

"I do." Audrey couldn't remember going over those details in her interview, but if he had glanced at her employee information, it was there to be seen.

"I live in Brentwood, you're on the way, and I'm headed home. Why don't you let me take you?"

"Oh, I couldn't do that. I don't want to impose."

"So I'm just supposed to leave you here stranded in my parking lot?" Troy's grin was lopsided, and Audrey liked the way his brown eyes twinkled as he teased her. The thought of riding in the same vehicle with Troy for the next twenty-five minutes sent butterflies skimming along her nerves.

"You do have a good point. I'd love a ride."

"We probably have about fifteen minutes before he gets here. I suggest we wait inside the office." Troy walked to the door and held it open for Audrey.

"Thank you." She stepped past him into the cool office interior. Troy's phone rang and he answered, lifting a finger as he stepped into his office. Audrey pulled out her own phone and called LuAnne, explaining the car trouble and making sure keeping the girls a bit longer wouldn't be a problem. By the time she got off the phone, the tow truck had arrived. Audrey handed the mechanic her keys and gave him her information, and when Troy joined her in the parking lot, her car was just going around the corner.

"That was fast. I'm glad he could get here so quick," Troy observed.

"Probably had something to do with who called him. Thank you for that," Audrey replied.

Troy grinned. "Right this way." He motioned to a shiny silver Mercedes parked under an ash tree in the only shade on the parking lot. He went around to the passenger side and opened the door for her.

Audrey hesitated before climbing inside. She looked at Troy and smiled. "Thank you very much."

Her ex-husband Drew had stopped opening the door for her as soon as they were married. At the time, she bought into

Drew's explanation for his lack of chivalry—that she was a strong, independent woman who didn't need someone to baby her. Later, when they had two kids and she could've used someone to look out for her, she had begun to realize just how little Drew actually cared for her. She slid into the sleek interior of Troy's car, noticing the cool leather seats and tinted windows.

Troy pushed a button to start the car and eased out of his parking space. "Mike stopped by my office earlier today. He wanted to know if I thought you were ready to take on a new client in addition to Felicia."

Audrey tightened her grip on her purse, realizing this could be an impromptu job interview. She swallowed. "I definitely can handle more clients. I've been a vocal coach for many years and had up to a dozen students before. I know the caliber I'm working with now is different, but I love teaching, and being in the studio gives me an idea of what you're looking for."

Troy nodded. "That's what I told Mike."

"Thank you," Audrey said.

"So next week he'd like you to start working with Jake Mendez."

"Jake Mendez? As in Jake from Seven Arrows?" Audrey leaned forward, gaping at Troy.

Troy chuckled. "That's the one. I'm sure you understand, but it doesn't matter how great a vocalist you are, you can always use lessons, practice, and new techniques to improve the vitality of the voice."

Audrey could've leaned over and kissed Troy for understanding just how vital her position was for a vocalist. "I do. It's just, I've been a fan of his for a long time." Audrey leaned back in the seat. "It would be an honor to work with him."

"I'm glad to hear that. Jake has complained of his voice getting a little tired when he's on tour, and he wants to learn some new strengthening exercises." Troy kept one hand on the steering wheel and one hand on his knee, tapping to an unseen beat.

"Has music always run through your veins?" Audrey asked.

Troy's hand stilled and he glanced at her, his eyes softening. "I think it has. For a long time in my life, I couldn't hear any music at all, but it's always been with me. It's a great source of comfort and inspiration. I start every day and end every day with music."

Audrey remembered when she'd been the same way. Her entire life had been layered with melody upon melody. She loved singing, dancing, playing the piano, writing music, and finally teaching it. It wasn't until she'd been married to Drew for five years that she felt her connection with music slipping. Drew was like a discordant tone to her melody. She could never find the right harmony with him—like they were always singing off-key. "Since my divorce, I feel like the music has come back even stronger into my life," Audrey said, and then worried that she'd shared too much.

"I bet you're glad to have the music back. I think I understand what you mean." Troy glanced at her and then back at the road. "I sure am glad you found your way to Nashville."

Audrey felt the back of her neck tingling, and she imagined her cheeks were pink under Troy's sincere compliment. "My girls have done really well since moving here. Their father didn't want anything to do with them, and rather than live close by the hurt, we moved. I had no idea we'd fall in love with the city so quickly."

"It's unfortunate that those sorts of circumstances brought you here, but I'm glad you made it. I love it here," Troy said. "People around here are some of the best in the world."

"I agree." Audrey admired him as he drove. His arms were bronzed from the sun, and his dark hair had a bit of wave to it. He carried himself with a confidence and power that Audrey wished she had. She was working on it, but Troy seemed at ease no matter where he was.

"So where in Franklin do you live?" he asked.

"Echo Estates," Audrey replied. "It's right by those two Mormon churches—well, one of them is the temple. It's really pretty."

Troy nodded. "I know the one. Beautiful area, quiet too."

"We were lucky to find a home there," Audrey said.

They drove down a winding tree-lined road, and Troy shook his head. "I'm on autopilot, I guess. I'm sure there is probably a more direct route to Franklin, but we'll go right past the turnoff to my house."

"Oh, I don't mind," Audrey said. "I've driven this road a few times. Brentwood seems like a beautiful city."

"It is. I'm very lucky to live there. I didn't grow up around here," Troy said.

"Oh? Where did you grow up?"

"Just outside of Memphis. Small town. My daddy and mama worked hard. Did everything they could to help me get to college. I made some pretty good investments early on and made my first million by age twenty-two."

"Wow, that's impressive." Audrey appreciated how easy Troy was to talk to. He sounded humble and sincere when he talked about his success. "I hope it's appropriate to ask you, but is it true you're a billionaire?"

Troy chuckled. "It is true. One of the best days in my life was when I bought my daddy a brand-new pickup truck."

Something about the way he spoke softened Audrey's heart. He wasn't bragging, and she liked that. It was obvious that he truly had loved the moment he'd been able to get his parents a new vehicle. "That's wonderful to do something so nice for your parents."

"That's nothing compared to what they did for me," Troy replied. They continued down the beautiful tree-lined highway until Troy slowed. "Right up here is where I live. Do you see the gate? That's the entrance to my property."

"I bet it's lovely."

"It is. Definitely bigger than I ever thought I'd have and more than I need now, but there's always the future."

Audrey heard more than he said; his words were tinged with sadness. She knew that money didn't make people happy, but it had always seemed like she'd be a whole lot happier with more. Here she was, sitting right next to a billionaire in his Mercedes, and as he pointed out his large empty mansion just beyond the iron gates, she could clearly see that he was lonely.

"This area has a lot of good schools. I'm thankful for that." Audrey smiled, carefully changing the subject away from Troy's hint at the future.

"Well, Tennessee is pretty low on the totem pole of education, but you're right—there are some good schools and teachers out there."

"I'd like to hold on to the summer, though. It always goes by too fast," Audrey replied.

"You know what I love most about this time of year? Early June, that is." Troy turned to her.

"No, what is that?"

"Lightning bugs. I loved 'em ever since I was a kid. I bet your daughters were surprised to see them the first time."

Audrey smiled. "We love them. It's so fun to see them come out each night. My Lizzie still thinks that they're Tinkerbell's friends."

Troy chuckled. They continued to talk all the way until Troy pulled into her driveway and cut the engine. The sun had set by the time they reached her home, and Audrey wished that the drive was just a bit longer so she could keep talking to Troy.

"Thanks again for bringing me home." Audrey reached for her door handle.

"Wait, let me get your door for you." Troy jumped out before she could protest, dashed around his car, and opened her door.

"Thank you." She took his offered hand as she stepped out of the car. She tried not to think about how she was holding hands with her boss, who was also a billionaire and standing in front of her house. He had gone out of his way to help her and make her feel comfortable, and she didn't want to say goodbye.

"Speaking of Tinkerbell's friends." Troy pointed at the bushes around her house. "The lightning bugs are already coming out."

Audrey squinted, and sure enough she saw a flicker of light. "Wow, they're early tonight."

"I remember chasing lightning bugs when I was a kid. My brother and I would capture them in a jar, and my mom always told us to let them go. She told this story about how they were God's guiding lights for little boys looking for too much trouble." Troy chuckled. Then he stopped abruptly and looked at Audrey. "Sorry, I keep forgetting that you have a sore spot with God."

Audrey shook her head. "Obviously I don't mind, because I work for a Christian music company. You may have heard of them—Arise Music?"

Troy grinned and leaned back against his car. "I think I have heard of them. They've been around for a while, but about ten years ago some slick kid took over the business. I heard he was really handsome."

Audrey gave his shoulder a push, tipping him off balance. "I did hear he was handsome in his younger days. But as he got older, it always looked like he needed a good haircut." She reached out and ruffled the hair that always fell across his forehead. Troy grabbed her hand, laughing, and then stilled when their eyes met.

The heat of the day had packed into the concrete and simmered up to her fingertips. She didn't look away; instead, she drank in every one of his smile lines. His hand was warm against her skin.

"I like talking to you, Audrey," Troy said. He loosened his grasp on her arm and trailed his fingertips down along her wrist and across her hand. All he was doing was touching her arm and her hand, but the moment had turned from playful banter to an emotional connection that begged for more.

"I know I shouldn't, but I wondered if maybe we could forget that I'm your boss and you could go out to lunch with me sometime?" Troy asked.

Audrey pressed her teeth against her bottom lip. She could still feel the ghost of his fingertips on her arm, and she wanted more. "Well, you're the boss, but don't you have rules against those types of things?"

"I don't think it's written in stone." Troy shrugged. "And I am the boss."

"In that case, I might consider it," Audrey said. Her nerves were exploding like fireworks on the Fourth of July, and even though a part of her warned that maybe this wasn't a good idea, when she looked into Troy's chocolate-brown eyes, she couldn't resist. She studied him, thinking that he seemed like any other ordinary guy she might meet. There was nothing about him besides his nice clothes and nice car that gave proof to his billionaire status. She liked how approachable and down-to-earth he was.

"I'd like to know what's going on under that red head of yours," Troy said.

Audrey blushed and looked down at the ground. Then she raised her eyes to his. "I was just thinking how you seem like a regular guy, and I like that."

Troy pressed his fingers against hers. "I am a regular guy. I don't often get a chance to be relaxed enough for people to see it. I really appreciate how you brought that out in me today. It means a lot to me that you listen, and you aren't afraid to ask questions about me."

Audrey was flattered by his words, and every one of them felt sincere. It was so unlike her interactions with Drew. Her ex-husband would give her compliments, but every one of them felt slimy and hitched to expectations—she hadn't seen Drew clearly until he broke her heart. "I feel the same way." She squeezed his fingers in return and when he let go of her hand, she immediately missed his warmth.

"How will you get back to Nashville tomorrow? I'd offer you a ride, but I have some early-morning meetings."

Audrey shook her head. "Thank you, but I'm pretty sure my neighbor can help me out. She has my girls now and her husband works in Nashville."

"Okay. I guess I'd better get going and let you go get your girls." Troy straightened and stepped away from his car. "I hope you're still planning on coming to the company picnic. I'd like to meet the rest of your family."

Audrey nodded. "I think we'll make it."

"I'll see you tomorrow. Be sure and let me know if you have any trouble with your car."

"I will. Thanks again, for everything." Audrey waved as Troy backed out onto her road and drove away. As he drove, lightning bugs flickered in succession just behind his car, almost as if signaling that Audrey should follow him. She smiled and shook her head. It was fun to flirt, and it was nice that she got along well with Troy, but maybe she shouldn't go out with him. God was everywhere in his life, so present that Troy even mentioned Him when talking about lightning bugs. Audrey had put up walls around her heart after her divorce, keeping God out of everything. Now, standing on her driveway, watching the lightning bugs rise and fall along the beautifully manicured lawns, a tiny part of her heart whispered that maybe it was time to forgive.

Audrey received a call early the next morning that her car would be ready in a couple hours. It had been something to do with the alternator, as Troy had guessed. Secretly, Audrey was grateful for the car trouble. The time she'd spent with Troy was something she would savor for days.

She was able to get a ride to work with LuAnne's husband, Dwayne, and when Audrey walked into Arise Music, it was with expectation at seeing Troy's smile and maybe having a few minutes to chat. She was disappointed to learn from Rachel that Troy had been called out of town for an emergency and wouldn't be back for the rest of the week. It was probably better that way. It made it easier for Audrey to concentrate on the preparation work she would need to do for her first session with Jake Mendez.

She spent a lot of time going over his songs and recordings, listening to him live and in studio. His first appointment wouldn't be until after the company picnic, and hopefully Audrey would have a chance to meet him there. In the meantime, she had logged nearly twenty hours of work, but all of her research helped her notice things that would also help Felicia and other singers. At times, it almost felt like she was being led to notice things she hadn't before. She didn't allow herself to follow that thought too closely; she just kept working and thinking about Troy every few minutes.

Chapter 5

The day before the company picnic, Audrey's middle was a ball of nerves. She wanted to go, and at the same time she wanted to stay home. For the past week, whenever she passed Troy in the office, her stomach had flipped every time he smiled or looked her way with his chocolate-brown eyes. When she told LuAnne she was thinking of staying home because it was awkward to be around all of the happy families as the single divorcee, LuAnne insisted that Audrey was going, and she would go with her.

"You think I'm gonna let you miss out on seeing all those music stars and taking me with you?" she'd asked.

Audrey was grateful for a good friend. On Monday night, she drove to LuAnne's house and picked her up. LuAnne had a bounce to her step as she walked down the driveway. She opened the door and smiled as she slid in the car. "I feel only a tiny bit guilty for leaving Dwayne with the kids." She put her index finger and thumb close together. "But only a tiny bit."

Audrey chuckled. "You're the best, Lu. I'm glad you could come."

"What are friends for?" Lu turned to the back seat. "Are y'all excited to meet the famous musicians?"

"Mommy said we have to be good," Lizzie said.

"Well, that won't be too hard for you two girls."

"I might be a famous singer someday," Katie said.

"If you sing anything like your mama, you will be," LuAnne replied.

Audrey drove into Nashville and headed to Belmont University, where the party would be held. She and the girls had been to the Belmont Mansion when they first moved to Nashville. Audrey had definitely enjoyed the tour more than the girls, but she'd always had a weakness for history and great stories. The mansion was nearly two hundred years old and had been fully restored, open to the public for tours. The tour guides knew extensive details about Adelicia Acklen's interesting life as one of the richest women in the South during the 1800s.

Audrey thought that Belmont University was something out of a dream. The opportunity for students to learn music and business and have access to so many doors open to their talent right in the heart of Nashville was pretty fantastic. They walked the campus together, Lu holding Katie's hand and Audrey holding Lizzie's. It took them a few minutes to find the location of the private party on a patio overlooking the green. Audrey's stomach clenched as she noted that there were over a hundred people in attendance.

Even though she told herself not to, Audrey couldn't help but scan the crowd for Troy. She was interested to see who his date would be. But as they made their way to an empty table and sat down, there was still no sign of their host.

Audrey commanded herself to stop looking and focus all of her attention on her kids and her friend. Just as the first salad plates were being served, several heads turned toward the front of the patio. Audrey followed their gaze until she saw Troy Jackson standing there with a smile on his face.

"Thank y'all for coming out tonight. It's an honor to work with all of you. I know we're all hungry, so I won't be giving a long speech; just make sure you save room for dessert, which includes the cupcake walk. You know you don't want to miss that one." Laughter rippled through the open patio, and Troy smiled. "Enjoy your meal."

Troy moved to a table near the front and sat down, but there were several people in the way, so Audrey couldn't see who he was sitting next to. She reminded herself that she didn't care, because he was her boss and he should be there with a beautiful woman as his date.

"Audrey, if you don't stop looking over there so hard, you're going to get a neck ache," LuAnne whispered.

Audrey closed her eyes and then opened them and refocused on her plate. "I'm just looking to see if Felicia is here," Audrey lied.

"Uh-huh, I bet you are," LuAnne said.

Audrey narrowed her eyes. "There are a lot of famous people here. See anyone you know?"

"It only took me about ten seconds to spot Jake from Seven Arrows."

Katie perked up. "He's here? Where?"

Audrey and LuAnne both pointed three tables over, where the lead singer of the Seven Arrows band was eating next to his wife.

"Mommy, I want to meet him. Can I get his autograph?" Katie asked.

"After dinner let's see if we have a chance to talk to him." Audrey hadn't told anyone about the upcoming opportunity to work with Jake. It seemed like if she spoke it aloud, she'd realize it was all a dream.

"This food is so pretty," Katie said. She picked up a mini chicken croissant sandwich and took a bite. Katie reached into the wicker basket in the center of the table, where an assortment of cheese and crackers were displayed. Another platter held shish kabobs made of fresh fruit.

"I love my bob," Lizzie said. She held a skewer of pineapple and grapes and waved it back and forth before sliding off a purple grape.

The food was delicious, definitely a far cry from regular picnic fare. But everyone looked at ease, wearing casual clothing and interacting with friends and family. Felicia sat next to her boyfriend, who looked a little rough around the edges, but she was smiling and so was he.

When Lizzie asked to use the bathroom, Audrey jumped at the chance to stand up and weave her way through the tables, catching a glimpse of Troy. He was sitting next to a much older beautiful woman who appeared to be his mother. His father was there too. Audrey recognized him from the photo in Troy's office. She felt relief and curiosity that Troy didn't have a date. Was he too busy to date? Audrey had to wonder. Or maybe he wanted to stay focused at his company party.

On their way back from the bathroom, Audrey's eyes wandered over to Troy's table again. He looked up just at that moment, catching her eye and inclining his head toward her. She smiled, nodding, and as she passed the neighboring table, she heard someone say Troy's name and a mumbled "He never brings a date to the company parties."

Audrey steered Lizzie back to their table and felt heat rushing to her cheeks. She didn't know much about Troy, but apparently the guests here expected him to come to the company party with his parents. She sat down and took a long drink of iced tea.

"I saw you ogling your boss again," LuAnne whispered.

"Okay, I'll admit it. I have a crush on him." Audrey decided it was best to come clean. She did have a crush on Troy, but that was all. Who wouldn't have a crush on him? He was as handsome as they come, sincere, and loaded, but she definitely wasn't his type. He had never been married as far she could tell, and what man would want to be saddled with a woman nearing forty who had two kids? "I just need to get him out of my system. He's just a shiny new toy, that's all."

LuAnne gave her a knowing look. "If you say so."

"I do." Just then, the servers brought out strawberry cheesecake drizzled with chocolate, and that was enough to take anybody's attention away from Audrey and her crush.

Around the time the servers were clearing the dessert plates, music started up, and Audrey recognized it as one of the hits from Seven Arrows. She looked over to see Jake smile and wink at his wife. People started getting up and mingling with other tables. In the grassy area there were games set up for families with cornhole toss, horseshoes, and even a little putting green.

Several children cheered when the servers brought out cupcakes on three-tiered stands. Lizzie pulled on Audrey's hand. "Mommy, the cupcake game. Come on!"

They hurried over to the edge of the sidewalk, and Lizzie and Katie both jumped on a colored mat that had a number monogrammed on it. A dozen more children joined the game and the music started. Just as the kids began walking around the circle, Troy hopped on a mat, and everyone cheered as he hopped to the next mat. The music stopped and Troy scrambled for a mat in between Lizzie and another little boy. Audrey laughed along with several others as numbers were called out and Troy helped hand out cupcakes to the winners.

Audrey told herself not to stare, but the boyish look of happiness on Troy's face was too endearing to miss. He looked right at home with the kids, who giggled and pointed when he stumbled to find a number every time the music stopped. Within a few minutes, all of the kids were winners, and extra cupcakes were nabbed by their parents. Katie and Lizzie returned, grinning with their cupcakes. Lizzie had pink icing smeared across her cheek and half of the cupcake gone. Each cupcake had three glowing bracelets around the base.

"Look, Mommy! Glow stick bracelets!" Lizzie said as she pulled the bracelets off and put them on her arm.

Katie pulled hers off as well, smiling as she jiggled the green, pink, and yellow bracelets. "Look, Lu!"

"You two can light the way home tonight," LuAnne replied. She turned to Audrey and tilted her head. "That is pretty cool that he would do that for the kids."

Audrey nodded and looked over to where she'd last seen Troy. He was surrounded by kids hugging his legs and others showing him their bracelets. Several people approached Troy, and they stood and talked with smiles on their faces. Audrey grabbed LuAnne's hand and gave it a quick squeeze. "Thanks so much for coming with me. Around this time is when I really start feeling like a sore thumb."

"You're not the only single one here," LuAnne replied. "There's your boss, for one."

Audrey nudged LuAnne with her elbow. "Quit teasing, you'll make it worse."

LuAnne chuckled. "Okay, I will, but you should know he's heading this direction."

Audrey gasped. "Don't tease me."

LuAnne gave her head a little shake. "I'm not," she whispered.

Audrey's skin tingled—Luanne was serious. She turned her head just as Troy joined their circle.

"I'm really glad to see you made it," Troy said. "I've been looking forward to meeting your family."

"Thank you. This has been a wonderful party, and I really don't think it qualifies as a picnic," Audrey said. She smiled, hoping that Troy couldn't hear the thumping of her heart in her chest. Lizzie reached up and squeezed her hand. Her youngest daughter always seemed to sense when Audrey was nervous. Audrey swallowed and smiled down at her daughter. "These are my daughters, Lizzie and Katie."

Troy held out his hand. "I'm pleased to meet you. So let's see … Katie, you must be about ten, right?"

Katie seemed to grow an inch under his gaze. "I'm nine," she replied. Troy had won her over without even trying.

"I'm six," Lizzie replied. "And the cutest!"

Audrey shook her head as Troy laughed. "I don't know about that, Lizzie. It's a tough race between you and your sister and your mama."

"This is my friend, LuAnne Clark." Audrey launched into the next introduction, hoping that her face wasn't in flames.

"Happy to meet you." Troy shook LuAnne's hand.

"Same to you," LuAnne replied. "You're all Audrey talks about. She loves working for you."

Audrey nudged LuAnne with her foot, gritting her teeth. "LuAnne is the assistant principal at my kids' school. She's been helping out this summer with tending them."

"So tell me this, LuAnne," Troy asked. "Do you ever dare to play Frisbee with Audrey?"

LuAnne laughed so hard she snorted. That made Troy laugh harder, and Audrey and the girls joined in.

"No fair, Duke isn't here to defend me," Audrey said.

"Well, I told you I wanted another chance to meet him. I'd like to hear his side of the story." Troy arched one eyebrow, and Audrey couldn't believe that he was flirting with her at his company party.

"You ought to join Audrey for one of her morning runs with Duke," LuAnne said. "Don't you live over in Brentwood?"

Troy nodded. "Impressive. Your friend here has done her homework."

LuAnne rolled her eyes. "Not hard to do. Doesn't everyone in Nashville know where you live after that article they ran a couple years ago?"

Troy's face went slack.

LuAnne covered her mouth. "I'm sorry! I put my foot in it. Please forgive me."

Troy wiped his forehead. "No problem. Well, I hope you enjoy the rest of the night. I'll chat with you later."

He turned and walked away. Before he could even get ten paces away, LuAnne grabbed Audrey's arm. "I'm so sorry. I didn't even think."

"What do you mean?" Audrey asked. "What are you talking about? Why is he so upset?"

"It was two or three years ago," LuAnne replied. "This singer, they wanted to be part of his record company, and Troy didn't like his demo. Things turned nasty, and the guy set a cross on fire in Troy's yard."

Audrey gasped. "That's awful! Why would you bring that up?"

LuAnne shook her head. "You know how my mouth runs away from me. I'm going to apologize again. I'll make things right."

And before Audrey could respond, LuAnne was striding through the crowd after Troy.

"Mommy, I want to play cornhole," Lizzie said, waving toward an open beanbag board.

"Me too," Katie said.

It never ceased to amaze Audrey how children could be totally oblivious to a torrential hailstorm of emotions going on around them. She sighed. There wasn't anything she could do to stop LuAnne or salvage the situation on her own, so she might as well play with the girls.

Fifteen minutes passed and nearly five rounds of cornhole, and LuAnne still hadn't returned. Audrey scanned the crowd and found her talking with three or four people. LuAnne was definitely a social bug. Audrey didn't mind; her friend would find her way back eventually.

Audrey saw Jake Mendez and his family across the park and wished she could approach him, but with LuAnne gone and Troy upset, there was no one to help make an introduction. She was too nervous to attempt it on her own. It was probably better that way. She didn't want him to get the wrong impression and then cancel their upcoming session.

The kids flipped out when they identified a man and a woman tying balloons in extravagant designs. They got in line, and Audrey tried not to think about the look on Troy's face, the hurt in his eyes before he'd walked away. After they'd waited in line for twenty minutes, the girls were starting to get tired, but a mermaid balloon and dog balloon cheered them up. They went through a treat bar, lined with glass canisters of all kinds of candies, chocolates, dried nuts, and fruit. Audrey helped each of her girls load up a paper sack with treats.

"Let's sit down right here." She motioned to a spot underneath a magnolia tree. In some places the branches reached almost to the ground.

Audrey sat, closed her eyes, and inhaled deeply. Before moving to Nashville, she'd never seen a magnolia tree in real life, and the scent was something that couldn't be reproduced. Audrey loved it. She sat that way for a minute or two, until she heard someone sit next to her. She turned, fully expecting it to be LuAnne, and jumped back when she saw Troy.

"Oh, you startled me."

"I'm sorry about that. I didn't mean to sneak up on you." Troy leaned back on his hands. "I love the sultry smell of the magnolias this time of year."

"Me too. The girls and I planted a few on our property, but they have a ways to go before any of them will blossom."

"I won't mention how many I have on my property. You'll think I'm a fanatic."

"Well, now you have to tell me." Audrey leaned toward him.

"I think the last count was twenty-nine. There's a line of them coming up to the house."

"I'd like to see that sometime," Audrey replied without thinking.

"I'd like to show you." Troy's voice was soft and soothing. "Your friend, LuAnne, she's a spectacular gal."

Audrey wasn't sure how to respond to that. The last interaction he'd had with her spectacular friend hadn't ended well. She trailed her fingers through the grass, keeping an eye on Lizzie and Katie as they picked through their treat bags.

"She found me and apologized, told me she was mortified that she brought that up." Troy sat up, suddenly only six inches from Audrey's face. "I want you to know I don't harbor any resentment over that. It just took me off guard. I hadn't thought of it for a long time, and sometimes those old stories crop up and take me by surprise."

"You don't have to explain," Audrey said.

Troy covered her fingers with his own. "But I wanted to, because it looked like you didn't know what she was talking about. LuAnne said she told you a little bit about it. I just want you to know there's a lot more to that story than was in the news, and it's okay. We were able to work things out so that person could have a second chance."

"What do you mean? Why give him another chance to hurt someone?" Audrey asked.

Troy gave her fingers a gentle squeeze. "That's what most people would say, but I knew it was just a misunderstanding. I knew we could do better than jail time and exorbitant fines. So we worked it out."

Audrey watched him closely. His hair was getting a little long around the ears trailing down the side of his temple, his eyebrows were thick and dark. She had the sudden urge to trace his left eyebrow and touch his temple again, like she did when she'd hit him in the head with the Frisbee. She smiled. "You're a good man, Troy Jackson."

Troy met her gaze, his eyes growing darker. "I try every day. Thanks for noticing."

Audrey could feel his fingers on hers, the tips hot against her skin, sending sparks up her arms. Her heart beat in her throat, and the connection she'd felt before with him intensified. If she was smart and wanted to keep her job, she would keep her distance, but there was something about the way Troy looked at her that made her pause.

"Audrey, how would you feel if I joined you for a run with Duke?"

Audrey's heart jolted. Was he asking her out? "Well, I go nearly every morning, pretty early, but I could probably rearrange things for your schedule."

"How early?"

"Six o'clock. I have a neighbor girl that comes over. She loves reading, and she sits there and reads until I get back just in case my girls wake up."

"I can be there, if it's okay with you."

Audrey hesitated, wondering just how much he wanted to go for an early walk. Troy watched her with a smile, waiting for her answer. "You can park in my driveway and I'll be out at six."

"Can I come tomorrow, then?" Something about the way he asked made him seem even more attractive.

"That'd be fun." Audrey did her best to keep her voice normal. She turned her hand over and squeezed Troy's fingers as she said, "But I'll leave the Frisbee home."

Troy laughed and held her hand for another moment. "Tomorrow, then." He stood slowly and ducked back out from under the magnolia tree.

Audrey sat there for a few minutes, mentally pinching herself, wondering if she had just been dreaming. It wasn't until they all loaded up in the car and were on their way home that she told LuAnne what had happened. LuAnne squealed and clapped her hands, Audrey knew it wasn't a dream, and she might just be in more trouble than she'd bargained for.

Chapter 6

The next morning at 5:50, Troy parked in front of Audrey's house and did a few stretches while he waited. He heard Duke yip when they came out of the house, and Troy looked up. Audrey smiled brightly, and he felt more awake than he had been in years. She wore black and red running pants with a white shirt, and her hair was pulled back in a ponytail. She looked good—too good this early in the morning.

"Hi there. Hey, Duke." Troy held his hand out palm upwards in front of Duke's nose, letting the dog sniff him. Duke's ears perked up, and he licked Troy's hand.

"You're sure I shouldn't grab the Frisbee?" Audrey teased.

He laughed. "Not today. Are you ready?"

Audrey lifted her hand, and Duke's leash jingled. "I like to run for a mile and then walk the rest of the way."

Troy sucked in a mouthful of air and stretched his arms over his head. "I'm ready. It's been too long since I took time for a morning run."

They set off together down the bike path, Troy running on Audrey's right so Duke could trot along on her left.

"Mike told me you spent a lot of time last week prepping for Jake's first session. What kind of things do you look for?"

"I didn't know Mike had noticed. But yes, I have spent a lot of time studying." Audrey held Duke's leash loosely as she jogged. "I look for weak spots, places where I can hear the voice getting tired. I also listen for weak notes, especially where the singer transitions over the bridge."

Troy nodded. The point where the voice moved from high to low was often called a bridge, and it took a lot of practice to make a smooth transition without cracking. "You really do know your stuff."

"I know I shouldn't be nervous, but I still am." Audrey's words were punctuated by her increased breathing rate as they continued to run.

"Jake is as down-to-earth as they come. I've known him for several years, and he was really patient with me before." Troy stopped; he had been about to say something about his past. "Before I really got into the Christian music scene."

Audrey turned to him. "So you weren't always into Christian music? What made you decide to get into the business?"

"Arise Music was struggling when I came on board." Troy wondered how much he should share, because it was obvious Audrey didn't know anything about his past. "I felt called to a mission—to be an influence for good, something I never had when I was young. So I bought out the previous owners and immediately dumped several clients and took on new ones. I made a lot of waves, and people were pretty upset, but it's what needed to be done."

Audrey nodded. "I heard some of the details. It seems most people have good things to say about you and what you did for Arise."

Troy grinned. "Now they do. Five years ago it was pretty rough."

"What were you doing before then?"

"Besides being young and naïve?" He smirked. "Even before I got my head on straight, I made several investments. I lucked out and was pretty successful, but it wasn't the right path for my life." Troy kept things vague, hoping that Audrey's questions wouldn't delve too much deeper. It was refreshing that she didn't know all about his past. Most people he met knew his history, the tabloids, the exaggerated reports of his behavior, and every glaring mistake that had made headline news.

"Well, I'm sure people say this all the time, but you seem like a regular, hard-working guy to me."

"Thanks. That's what I want to be. I am a regular guy, and I want a regular life."

"Are you sure about that?" Audrey chuckled. "If I were you, I'd be eternally grateful for that maid and gardening staff you must have on hand."

Troy laughed. "That's true. There are some areas of my life that I don't want to be regular."

When they grew short of breath, they continued running in a comfortable silence. Troy didn't want to admit that he was a little more out of shape than he thought. He kept up with

Audrey just fine, but her pace was steady and even while his felt jerky.

"Up ahead, that tree is where I always stop." Audrey pointed, and Troy was relieved to see that the tree was only a few hundred yards ahead of them

"It's nice being out here before the heat sets in." Troy wiped his forehead across his sleeve.

Audrey patted Duke's head. "It's my favorite part of the day. Helps me feel centered for the rest of the day."

They slowed to a brisk walk, and Troy noticed the things he'd always loved about growing up in Tennessee. The grass that grew wild everywhere pressed snug against the tree trunks, creating a shady and moist environment. The soft rays of the sun filtered through the trees overhead as they ran through a copse of dogwood and ash. Birds called overhead and the warm air brushed against his face.

Audrey's skin glistened with sweat, and her red hair swished back and forth in the ponytail. Troy was attracted to her, and an old familiar feeling reared up inside, but he breathed in and out, slowly recognizing that he was a different man now. He wasn't just attracted to Audrey physically; he was attracted to the person that she was, and he had a desire to get to know her better. But this was unchartered territory. Audrey didn't know about his past, and he didn't know her well enough yet to anticipate how she might react when she learned more about him. A strand of doubt wound its way through his core, and Troy wondered if it might be better just to let her be. But then Audrey turned and flashed him one of her endearing smiles, and he couldn't resist her.

"You must have a lot on your mind this morning," Audrey said.

"Fatal side effect of my job," Troy replied.

Audrey studied him. "I think your mind was further than your job, wasn't it?"

Troy nodded. "Can I be frank with you?"

"I prefer Troy because I know him a little better, but Frank's okay."

Troy hesitated, and then he laughed. Audrey joined him and let out a little snort, which made them both laugh harder. "That was a bad joke, but it was so funny for some reason."

"Hey!" Audrey pushed him off balance. "When you're practicing humor for a six- and nine-year-old, that's what you get."

"Okay, I'll just come out with it. I'd like the chance to get to know you better, but I'm guessing we both might have a little baggage. I'm wondering if this is the right place in your life to consider dating a guy like me."

"Duke, halt." Audrey gave a light tug on Duke's leash, and he stopped, turned, and sat next to her feet. She reached out and patted his head "Good boy." She looked up at Troy. "You're right, I do have a lot of baggage. I haven't really attempted to date since my divorce, so I'm probably not the best candidate for someone like you." She looked down at her feet.

Troy reached out and took her hand. "Actually, that's what I could say about myself. You seem like you have everything together. I'm thirty-five, and I've never been married. That's quite a disappointment to my mother, I'll have you know."

Audrey looked into his eyes and smiled. "Well, I'm willing to try dating, especially if it's someone as nice as you."

"The media hasn't been on my heels for the past year, but there's always that chance. I just don't want you to get hurt," Troy said. "You understand?"

Audrey's smile faltered. "I used to be really afraid of getting hurt, but now I think that's just part of life. I don't go looking for trouble, but I've survived the worst I could ever imagine. I think I could probably survive a few dates with you."

Troy frowned. "What did he do to you?"

Audrey swallowed. "He cheated on me multiple times. I never knew until he found a girlfriend he decided to keep."

Heat flashed through Troy's veins, and he felt his face burning with shame. This was the point where he should definitely tell Audrey that being friends was probably safer. But when he opened his mouth to speak and looked into her vivid blue eyes, he just couldn't do it. "I'm really sorry you had to go through that. I'm sorry that he treated you that way." He took her hand, noticing how small her palm was against his.

Audrey shrugged. "I can't change the past. I'm much happier now, but it took me a while to figure out that I'm the one in charge of my happiness."

"You sound much wiser than I feel," Troy replied.

"Maybe that's because I am." Audrey smiled.

Troy laughed. "I like how you can do that, be serious and then laugh about life."

"My two little girls make it a requirement for life," Audrey replied.

Troy still held her hand, and they pivoted and started back the way they'd come.

"So when can I take you out on our first official date?" Troy gave her hand a little squeeze. "Are you busy Friday?"

"I think that would work. What do you have in mind?"

"Definitely dinner. I'll come up with something."

"*Something* sounds wonderful. I'd love to go out with you," Audrey said. "Thanks for coming with me and Duke today."

They walked back to Troy's car, still holding hands. "Thanks again for this morning."

"I'll be in several meetings today, but I'll make sure I'm there for Jake's first session tomorrow."

"Okay. I'll see you then." Audrey looked like she was about to say something else, but she turned to Duke. "C'mon, boy."

Troy whispered a silent plea to the heavens. "Please, don't let my past ruin this chance."

When Troy walked into Arise Music later that morning, even Rachel noticed his mood.

"My, you look chipper today," she said.

Troy just nodded and headed to his office, where Mike was waiting. Troy groaned when he noticed Mike rubbing the top of his bald head, because that always meant some problem was on his mind. "Good morning."

"Troy, man, you're my bro, but what are you doing?" Mike asked as if they'd already been talking for five minutes.

Troy blinked, trying to catch up. "What do you mean?"

Mike rolled his eyes. "I saw you last night talking to Audrey. You two looked pretty cozy."

Troy swallowed. "I asked her out on a date."

Mike sighed and rubbed the back of his head. "Why would you do that? I thought you had all sorts of rules in place for these kinds of things."

Troy put his fingers into his hair, thinking of how Audrey had said he needed a haircut. He still hadn't had time to get to a barber, but it was at the top of his list. "I like her. She's different. She didn't act all weird about, well, you know, all the money stuff. There hasn't been any sort of expectations or requests. It seemed like she didn't really even notice."

"You mean that you're a billionaire?" Mike leaned against Troy's desk. "I think she's noticed. She knows you're one of the most eligible bachelors in Tennessee and pretty much untouchable. What I can't figure out is why you think she hasn't noticed."

"Well, yes, she noticed, but it was different because she came right out and asked me about it the first time we had a chance to talk. No one's ever done that before. Everybody just tries to pretend like the money isn't an issue because they're so worried about being perceived as a gold digger."

"That's because they are gold diggers. Maybe she's just figured out a new act."

"Mike, you're the one who brought her in here. Tell me you have more respect for her than that."

Mike lifted up his hands. "You're right. I did bring her in here—to work, not date you. This is just my regular response to any woman interested in you. I don't like seeing you hurt or used."

"It's been a long time since I've let anybody get close enough to do either of those." Troy hadn't dated anyone seriously in the past two years, much to his mom's chagrin. His past was rocky, and he'd done his share of using beautiful women who only were interested in his money. He had come close to losing everything before he finally decided to listen to God and change his life. It bothered him sometimes, seeing the worry on his parents' and friends' faces. It hurt knowing that Mike wasn't sure how long Troy would last on this new path. Troy sucked a breath in through his nose and breathed out through his mouth. "I'll be careful. I just want to have a chance to get to know her better. I hope you can support me in that."

Mike patted Troy on the back. "You know I'll support you. I'll do some more digging on her, of course," he chuckled. "But if you think she's different, I think so too."

"Thanks, Mike." Troy walked around the side of his desk and gazed out the window. "Seems like I never really get a chance. My past is always chasing me. My money ruins a chance at an authentic relationship. I don't mean to be the whiny rich kid, but sometimes life ain't fair."

Mike laughed. "You can complain all you want, just make sure I get a hefty bonus." He winked and walked out of Troy's office.

Troy stared out his window for about ten more seconds before his next appointment started. He couldn't wait to see Audrey again.

Chapter 7

On Wednesday morning, Audrey's pulse was humming with anticipation of seeing Troy again. He'd cured her nervousness over working with Jake Mendez, but then replaced it with a butterfly-filled anxiety of seeing her boss-turned-potential-boyfriend. She changed her outfit three times before settling on a teal blouse and white skirt with wedge sandals that gave her a good three inches over her regular five-foot-one height.

The girls were happy to be dropped off at LuAnne's again. "Thank you so much, Lu," Audrey said. "Once school starts, I'll be scheduling all of my coaching appointments during school hours so that the girls won't have to go to a sitter."

"You're lucky that they'll work with you like that," LuAnne replied.

"One of the perks of being a contract-based employee," Audrey said. "I get to set my own hours."

"Well, I won't keep you, but I expect a full report because, girl, you are glowing like a lightning bug."

Audrey grinned. "I'm just excited about life, that's all."

"Uh-huh, that's fo' sure." LuAnne infused more Southern drawl into her response.

"See you in five hours." Audrey waved and hurried out the door before LuAnne could ask any more questions.

Audrey made it to the office almost an hour before her session with Jake. She sorted through her notes, cued up some recordings, and tidied up the room. Just before ten o'clock, Troy entered with Jake in tow.

"Audrey Blair, meet Jake Mendez."

Jake had light brown skin and his black hair was shaved short on the side and spiky on top. He always seemed to look cool yet casual. He smiled as he shook her outstretched hand. "It's a pleasure to meet you. I've heard so many great things about you from Felicia."

Audrey shook her head and smiled. "I'm thrilled to meet you. I'm a big fan of your music. You're very talented." It was all she could do to keep from gushing, but Jake's grin only widened.

"I think Troy likes you. I've never heard him act this enthusiastic about a vocal coach before," Jake said.

Audrey's cheeks heated, and she turned from him as casually as she could. "Well, it took a lot of arm-twisting from Mike to even get me in here, so I won't argue with progress." She noticed that the tips of Troy's ears were pink. He winked at her and Audrey continued, trying to quiet the tribal dancers in her belly.

"Do you mind if I observe for a few minutes?" Troy asked.

"Not at all," Audrey answered sincerely. Troy's presence ignited a fire in her soul while at the same time sending a calming vibe through the room. She checked her notes. "I'd like to start by going over an analysis of some of your recordings. There are a few things I want to see if you'll notice."

Jake nodded. "Okay, I'm game for that."

Audrey pushed play, and they listened to the beginning refrain of one of Jake's upbeat songs. Then she paused the playback. "Right there, before you go into the first chorus. Did you hear how you were reaching for that G?"

"Yeah. Can you play that part again?"

Audrey nodded and hit play. She and Jake continued in a similar way for the next fifteen minutes. Troy was quiet, jotting a few notes on a notebook and occasionally glancing her way. Audrey had finished analyzing the first song with Jake and was moving on to the next when Troy stood. "This is fantastic, Audrey. You're really going to make a difference with this studio." He walked forward and clapped Jake on the back. "I can't wait to hear your new songs. I'll talk to you to later."

"Thanks, man," Jake said.

"Yes, thank you," Audrey said. She pulled her eyes from Troy's retreating figure, noticing again his lean, strong physique. But with a tiny shake of her head, she refocused on Jake's music and the session at hand.

The rest of the coaching session with Jake was one of the best that Audrey had ever experienced. She didn't know if it was because she'd worked so hard in preparation or if it had something to do with Troy's presence and the praise he'd given both of them before he left. It was probably a combination of both. Jake left the meeting eager and enthusiastic about her suggestions and the new songs he was planning to start recording next month in the studio.

Audrey took a few minutes to write more notes after the session ended. She found herself glancing at the door, wondering if Troy would return to check on how things went. But when the door opened, it was Felicia, wearing a bright red sundress and a smile to match.

For the next hour, Audrey was immersed in coaching Felicia, and at the end of her second session of the day, she felt even better.

Felicia hugged her. "Thank you so much. I can tell that my voice is improving already."

Audrey hugged her back. "I'm so glad that it's helping. It's such a pleasure to work with you. I love your attitude."

Felicia grinned. "I'll see you Friday."

After lunch, Audrey did more prep work for her next coaching session with Jake and Felicia on Friday. For now, she was only needed in the studio three times a week, and that worked perfect for her summer schedule at home.

At two o'clock, Troy walked into the studio office, knocking on the side of the doorframe. "Mind if I come in for a minute?"

Audrey's stomach tumbled and she stood, brushing her papers into a pile. "What can I do for you?"

Troy smiled. "You can believe me when I tell you that you're extremely talented and we're lucky to have you here."

Audrey ducked her head. "Thank you."

Troy touched her chin, pulling her gaze toward his. "Do I make you feel uncomfortable? I mean this morning. Are we okay here at work?"

"You're perfect. It really helped put me at ease, and the session with Jake was amazing."

Troy let his fingers trail along her jaw. He placed his hand on her cheek gently. "How about now? Comfortable?"

Audrey put her hand over his, feeling the warmth emanating through his fingers to her cheek and down to her toes. "I feel great."

Troy's eyes flicked to her lips and then back to meet her gaze. He smiled, and then carefully removed his hand and took one step away. "I just wanted to check on you and make sure that everything's going okay. I don't want to put any pressure on you, or affect your work negatively."

Audrey immediately felt the absence of his touch. "Today was a perfect day. If every day could be like today, I wouldn't have any worries at all."

"I'm glad to hear that. Would it work with your schedule on Friday if I picked you up at six o'clock for dinner?"

Audrey felt the fluttering start up again in her stomach. "I think that'd be a great idea."

"Good, I'll see you then."

When Audrey picked up Katie and Lizzie, LuAnne insisted that they come back for dinner that night so they could chat. "It's the only way I'm gonna pull that glow out of you," she'd said with a knowing smile.

So Audrey took the girls home, set up the sprinkler, and enjoyed the afternoon throwing a tennis ball for Duke. The girls squealed every time he ran through the sprinkler with them. She threw together a green salad and took it with them when they returned to the Clarks' home.

Dwayne opened the door for them. LuAnne's husband stood more than a foot taller than Audrey, his head was shaved, and his skin was several shades darker than LuAnne's. He was like the big brother Audrey never had. "I hear you've been keeping yourself busy," Dwayne said with an easy grin.

"I am. And it's everything I've dreamed of for years. I'm so excited," Audrey replied.

Dwayne led her into the kitchen, where LuAnne was pulling lasagna out of the oven. "Yep, she's glowing, but maybe it's just her dream job."

Audrey groaned. LuAnne had obviously filled her husband in on her suspicions. "Have you two been talking about me again?"

LuAnne rolled her eyes. "That's what friends do. Now this lasagna needs ten minutes to cool. Spill it."

Audrey scanned the backyard through the Clarks' beautiful patio window. Katie and Lizzie were playing with Davon and Whitney. "Okay, I'm glowing because I've been working for over ten years to build up my vocal coaching business and it's finally coming to fruition."

"How did your session with Jake Mendez go today?" LuAnne asked.

"It was amazing. Troy was there, and instead of being nervous, I just felt peaceful. I was able to get all of my thoughts across, and Jake latched on to my ideas. He's excited for our next session."

"Troy was there?" LuAnne asked. "He's the owner of the studios," she said to her husband.

"Yes, he likes to observe my work with new clients," Audrey replied.

"He must be a pretty powerful observer for that kind of smile," Dwayne said with a chuckle.

Audrey shook her head. "That might be the other part of my glow. Troy asked me out on a date."

LuAnne clapped her hands. "I knew it!"

"I thought that sort of thing wasn't allowed? Dating your boss, I mean," Dwayne said.

"Well, when your boss owns the company, I guess he can make his own rules," Audrey replied. She smiled. "He's really nice and so down-to-earth."

"Well, you must be pretty fantastic if he could forgive you for having a friend with both feet in her big mouth," LuAnne said.

"That's true." Audrey had been so relieved with how gracious Troy had been with LuAnne's *speak first, think later* approach.

"So you're going to go on a date with him?" LuAnne asked.

"He actually drove out here and joined me on my morning run with Duke yesterday." Audrey confessed.

"And you didn't tell me? What? Are you holding out on me, girl?" LuAnne came over and put her hands on Audrey's arms and gave her a little shake. "I'm going to start interrogating your girls if you're not more forthright with me."

Audrey laughed. "Okay, okay. You know me. I'm a little skittish, and I'm still trying to figure out if I should get my hopes up or not."

"Don't get your hopes up, but do go on a date with this guy if he's nice." Dwayne stirred up a pitcher of iced tea while Audrey helped LuAnne finish setting the table.

"Hopefully I'll have a chance to meet him for the second time and make a better impression," LuAnne said as she started cutting the lasagna. She paused and looked at Audrey. "Just don't overthink this. It's Troy Jackson, he's a billionaire, and he's never been married."

Dwayne gave LuAnne a look that Audrey couldn't quite discern. She wouldn't admit to them how excited she was for the date. "Okay, I won't get all worked up about it."

It was good advice not to get her hopes up, not to open herself up too much for what might only be a few dates, but at the same time, LuAnne's words left a bad taste in Audrey's mouth. Audrey was able to steer the conversation away from Troy Jackson and any potential dates for the rest of the evening, even if her mind kept returning to the memory of his hand holding hers.

Troy had said something about tabloids in the news not being after him so much in the last year. Audrey wondered if maybe she should look him up again to see what he was referring to. She'd researched Arise Music and Troy before she turned in her résumé, but nothing unsatisfactory had come up. She straightened her shoulders; anything worth finding out about Troy he would tell her himself as they got to know each other. The date with him tomorrow would be the perfect opportunity to ask questions about his past and find out if there was a reason to hope.

Chapter 8

Troy finally had to turn the clock around on his desk to keep from checking it every two minutes all day long on Friday. He couldn't wait for his date with Audrey. His first official date with her would start in just a few hours. His secretary, Rachel, had scheduled him to the hilt all day with barely room to breathe. Even so, he'd been late for one appointment because he made time to slip into the end of Felicia's coaching session with Audrey. Audrey had sensed him immediately, her eyes going to the back of the room, and she smiled. His presence seemed to affect her in a positive way, and Troy was glad to see her smile.

There was something about her that was different from any other woman he'd known. He kept thinking about her whenever they were apart. About one o'clock, Troy watched Audrey walk through the parking lot and head home to get ready for their date. He told her they might be coming back into Nashville for the evening, so he would pick her up at her house before six. Troy finished his last meeting and dashed out the door. He hoped to beat rush-hour traffic and get a few things ready. He hadn't told Audrey his specific plan in case he decided to change his mind at the last minute. He still felt confident as he drove through the beautiful tree-lined road toward his home. They were having dinner at his home in Brentwood, where there would be no one to intrude, no one to take pictures, or ask questions. That's what he and Audrey needed for their first date.

After he made sure everything was ready, he left with plenty of time to spare to pick up Audrey. He'd even asked Rachel for a few suggestions, and his bubbly secretary had come through. She'd picked up two fashion doll sticker books, one for each of Audrey's daughters. Troy carried the brightly wrapped gifts up to Audrey's doorstep and knocked on the door. A couple minutes later, the door swung open and Audrey greeted him with Duke trailing behind.

"You look fantastic." Troy leaned in and pecked Audrey's cheek. His hand trailed along her fingertips as he took in the sight of her. She wore a green and white striped sundress that went about mid-calf, and her strappy silver heels added a few inches to her tiny stature.

Audrey's cheeks turned pink and she smiled. "You look pretty fine yourself."

Troy grinned. He had dressed carefully for the night in a dark blue button-up shirt and khaki pants. It was nice to see the admiration in Audrey's eyes and know that it was coming from a sincere place in her heart. Even the way she looked was different than other women. She managed to look natural yet gorgeous at the same time.

"Girls, do you remember my boss Troy from the party we went to?"

"Mommy, he has presents! Are they for us?"

Audrey noticed the gifts and motioned for Troy to come in. "You didn't need to bring anything."

Troy shrugged. "I just thought it would be fun for them to have something to do while we're out. Is it okay if I give it to them now?"

Audrey nodded, and both the girls squealed.

Troy studied them for a moment, checking the nametag on the first gift wrapped in purple paper. "This one is for Katie—" He held out the present. "—and this one is for Lizzie." He handed Audrey's younger daughter a present wrapped in pink glitter paper.

"Thank you," Katie said softly as she carefully unwrapped the book.

For a moment, Troy was worried that maybe she was too old for the activity and sticker book, but then her face lit up.

"Mom, it's the sticker book I was showing you in the store!" She hugged it to her chest and smiled at Troy.

"I got one too!" Lizzie danced around in a circle, holding her sticker book up high.

Troy laughed, feeling something that was foreign to him. The gifts hadn't even cost thirty dollars total, but the girls were as happy as he'd seen some kids on Christmas. He'd have to thank Rachel later.

"That was really sweet of you. That's the perfect gift for my girls," Audrey said. She looped her arm through his and squeezed his bicep. The closeness sent a thrill through his middle.

"I'm glad you like them," Troy said.

"Girls, what do you say?" Audrey prompted.

"Thank you," the girls answered in unison.

Troy was just about to ask about a sitter when he heard a light knock at the door.

"Oh, thank goodness, that's the sitter." Audrey let go of his arm and walked toward the door. "Let me just give her a few instructions, if you don't mind waiting."

"No problem at all. I'll just check a few emails." Troy pulled out his phone and got to work. A teenage girl entered, carrying a bulging backpack, and as Audrey took her into the living room, Troy was again reminded of how young Felicia Perry was. This babysitter looked to be only a couple years her junior. He suddenly felt old and like he'd wasted too much of his life making bad choices. With a shake of his head, he remembered the promises that he'd made to himself about not dwelling in a pool of regret.

A few minutes later, Audrey met him in the front entryway. Her brow furrowed. "Are we still okay? I'm not making us late, am I?"

Troy reached for her hand. "We have all the time in the world. Are you ready?"

"I am, and I can't wait to find out where we're going."

Troy led her out to his Mercedes and helped her into the passenger seat. He took a deep breath before he sat in the driver's seat and started the engine. "I was a little worried about my plans and what you might think, but I hope you don't mind. We'll be dining in at my house tonight."

Audrey leaned forward. "I'd love to see your home."

Troy smiled, grateful that he'd decided to let Audrey step closer to his heart by showing her his home. "I've been looking forward to tonight so much. I've had a hard time concentrating at work."

Audrey grinned. "Me too."

"Don't tell Mike," Troy said. "He was worried about me dating you, basically threatened me that I better not mess anything up with his vocal coach."

Audrey laughed. "Don't worry. I finally have my dream job. I'm not going to mess it up."

"Really? Your dream job is working for me?" Troy waggled his eyebrows.

Audrey tilted her head to one side. "Well, I guess that was an extra bonus I didn't anticipate."

"All kidding aside, we're really lucky to have you. I hope you let me know if you need anything or if you have ideas about what we might need to do to improve things."

"Thank you. That means a lot." Audrey leaned back in the seat and let her fingers trail along the leather armrest.

Troy moved his hand to cover hers, and she turned her palm upwards, interlacing their fingers together. The simple movement made his temperature go up a few notches.

They chatted easily all the way to Troy's driveway. Audrey sucked in a breath as they passed through the gate and dropped down the hill into his expensive property. "Oh my goodness, I didn't realize your house was this big."

"It is a bit ostentatious, I know. But it's a good investment—at least, that's what my accountant told me." Troy glanced at Audrey, trying to read her thoughts.

"I can't wait to see inside."

Troy let out a breath, not realizing he'd been holding it until that moment. Her approval meant a lot to him, not in the sense of how successful he was, but in the sense that she agreed with the choices he'd made.

Troy pulled into the first bay of his five-car garage. "I want you to know that not all of these bays are filled with cars."

"Really? What do you keep in them, then?"

"Mostly old storage stuff from the recording studio. Would you like to go in through the front door or the side entrance?" Troy opened Audrey's door and took her hand.

"Whatever you'd like is fine with me."

"Then I'll take you in through my entrance." Troy kept hold of her hand and led her through the breezeway to the side entrance, which opened into an expansive mud room that led to the kitchen. Troy remembered the first time he'd walked through the house and noticed that the kitchen was larger than his parents' home. He waited to see what Audrey would say.

"This is amazing." She traced the edge of the granite countertops as they walked around the island.

"Thank you." The meal was already prepared and set aside in the dining room, and it looked like his staff had been busy because the kitchen was pristine.

Audrey gazed around the kitchen. "How many people staff this house?"

"There are eight full-time employees," Troy replied. "I also have a larger staff during different times of the year."

Audrey whistled. "It's impressive that they can keep everything running with only eight people."

"I only work with the best. I'm very blessed to enjoy the life I do."

"That's important." Audrey nodded. "Someone once told me, 'Do the thing you're best at. You should never feel guilty for living in a large house with a large staff, because every day you help touch thousands, even millions of lives with the music you produce.'"

Troy's throat tightened with emotion. In one sentence, this woman had touched him deeper than anyone he'd ever dated before. Troy pulled her close and hugged her to him. "You don't know how much that means to me."

Audrey hesitated, and then put her arms around his waist, hugging him tight. "I'm sorry if no one's ever told you that before, but it's true."

Troy's pulse thrummed in a hot rhythm under his skin. He wanted to hold Audrey like this and listen to her sweet words forever, but he carefully let go, stepped back, and took her hand. "Ready to eat?"

"You're the boss." Audrey winked. "But I would love to see all of your house, if that's on the tour for tonight."

"All right, we'll circumvent the dining room for now and take a quick tour of part of the house. I don't want your dinner to grow cold." Troy led her through the first floor of his mansion, showing her the guest quarters and pointing out a wing for a few of the full-time employees who lived there. Then he ascended the sprawling staircase and led her to the master bedroom, which took up half of the second floor.

"Do you like living here?" Audrey asked. She fingered the white and blue brocade duvet cover on his bed.

Troy watched her, heat rising in his chest as she touched his bed. He swallowed and focused on the question she'd asked. "Sometimes it feels like I don't spend very much time here,"

Troy replied. "But when I am here, I do enjoy it, although it is very quiet at times."

Audrey walked around the room, stopping at each of the six windows and staring out at the grounds. "It's beautiful and peaceful. And maybe a bit lonely too?" She turned to face him.

Her words pierced him to his core. "How do you do that? How do you see what no one else does?"

"Because it's the same thing I feel." Audrey put a hand over her heart. "I'll admit it's different from you because I have my girls, but there's an ache, an emptiness. At first I tried to fill it, until I realized that I couldn't."

Troy followed her into the bathroom, where she paused to look at the claw-foot bathtub, running her finger along the edge of the porcelain. Her words resonated with feelings that he'd kept hidden from the world. They were feelings he hadn't recognized in himself until five years ago when he changed his life. Before then, he'd been doing everything possible to fill the void, unsuccessfully. That void still remained and would always be there until the right person could complete him. That's what his pastor told him. That's what his mother had urged him to seek.

"Are you happy, then, Audrey?" Troy took two steps toward her, stopping to study her face.

She shook her head. "Yes and no. It took me a while to realize that there are unique stages of happiness. There are different places of contentment, and when Drew cheated on me, my whole world shifted. I couldn't find my footing for the longest time, so I hid away."

"And what would happen if someone found your hiding place, and coaxed you out of your shell?" Troy took her hand, pulling her closer to him.

Audrey swallowed, and some emotion he couldn't place flashed through her eyes. She lifted one shoulder and let it fall. "I suppose if it was the right person I might take a few steps out, see if I can find my balance again."

Troy nodded. He didn't want to push her or make her feel uncomfortable. So he tugged lightly on her hand. "Well, hold on tight, because I have quite a feast prepared for us tonight."

Audrey relaxed and followed him back down to the dining room. Troy's staff was aware of his approach and immediately began preparations to serve the meal. Troy pulled out Audrey's chair, and she sat lightly on the massive seat, barely taking up half the space with her tiny frame. Troy sat at the head of the table next to her, and he bowed his head. "Do you mind if I say grace?"

Audrey shook her head and closed her eyes. He gave a brief prayer, and after giving his thanks, he noticed that the tendon in Audrey's neck was tighter than before. He looked away and motioned for his head chef to begin.

Audrey swallowed back the bitterness that was ever-present when she had to listen to people thank God for the blessings in their life. She hadn't prayed in over two years, and things were turning out just fine for her. But she didn't begrudge Troy for practicing his religion. Living in Tennessee, in the Bible Belt, had taught her that religion was important to these folks, and she wasn't about to argue with anyone. She'd started softening, even coming to the conclusion that maybe God was in other people's lives, but for one reason or another, he had decided to leave Audrey to her own devices.

Troy smiled at her. "I hope you enjoy lobster. My chef is one of the best. And wait until you taste the cauliflower couscous he makes to go with it."

Audrey had never heard of cauliflower couscous, so she decided not to comment on that part of the meal, although she was excited to taste it. "I've only had lobster twice in my life, but both times it was delicious."

Troy beamed. "That's good to know. It was kind of a risk surprising you this way. I'm glad you're a good sport."

Two servers brought out a beautiful chopped green salad dotted with candied pecans, diced pineapple, and cubed ham. There was a sweet vinaigrette on the side, and Audrey was tempted to ask for the recipe after her first bite.

Audrey enjoyed every single one of the six-course meal that Troy had planned for her. The couscous was tender, flaky, and delicious, and the lobster was perfect. By the time they finished dining, talking easily between every course, it was already after eight o'clock. Troy lifted his hands over his head, stretched, and yawned. "Wow, that was delicious. I'm hoping now would be a good time for a walk around the gardens."

Audrey patted her stomach. "I definitely need to get moving after eating all of that wonderful food."

Troy stood and reached for her hand, helping her from her chair. She looped her arm through his, and they walked out of the dining room, leaving the dishes for his staff to take care of. For a moment as they walked through the house together,

Audrey thought she could understand how the upper class in Regency times felt, always having someone to look after their every need. She wondered for half a second what it would be like to live Troy's life.

His home was breathtaking. Every room was decorated with a designer's touch. It looked like a home out of a magazine, or one of those rich and famous tours Audrey liked to watch on TV. But the home lacked warmth, and for some reason, Troy didn't seem completely comfortable in his own space. Audrey figured it probably had a lot to do with the conversation they'd had in his bedroom. He was lonely, and who could blame him? He was nearing forty, the time when most men were settled down and raising their families.

He guided her through a set of French doors that opened up onto a sloping patio. Audrey's breath caught. "Oh, this is lovely."

Troy turned to her and smiled. "This is my favorite place."

He led her down the steps and the paved path that wound through the beautifully manicured lawn lined with a low hedge and dotted with colorful flowers. Audrey breathed in slowly, reveling in the scent of magnolias. She looked upwards. "There they are, your magnolia trees. This smells like heaven."

Troy chuckled. "That's fitting, because it is my little piece of heaven. Come here, you'll see why."

The lawn had to be over two acres of grass that butted up against the forest of trees, making it impossible for Audrey to gauge how many acres of property his home rested on. The path wound around a trio of magnolia trees and opened up onto a wide meadow with a white gazebo sitting next to a pond. "You have a pond too? Are there fish in it?"

Troy nodded. "I keep it stocked. Do you think you and your girls would like to come visit and go fishing?"

The beat of Audrey's heart increased. Troy was already speaking of seeing her again, and not just her, but her children as well. There had been a few times that men had expressed interest in her since her divorce. All she'd had to do was bring up the fact that she had two kids, and their enthusiasm waned. "They would love that. I used to love to go fishing as a girl. Can't say that I've done much of it as an adult."

"I think we should remedy that quickly," Troy said. He led her to the gazebo, and they stepped inside. He leaned against the railing overlooking the glassy surface of the pond, and Audrey joined him. While she watched, a fish jumped, sending ripples through the lake. Audrey let out a surprised giggle, and Troy put his arm around her. "Would it be too much to ask you and your girls to come over tomorrow night for some fishing? Unless you already have other plans."

"We would love to. I'm surprised you don't have other plans." Audrey nudged him with her shoulder. "Every time I see you around the office, you have your head down or you're on the run to another appointment."

Troy sighed. "It's something I've been working on for the past year. I'm way too busy, and I feel like life is passing me by." He straightened and his eyes twinkled. "But I'm learning that there are benefits to being a billionaire. I just need to hire more people. The trick is finding just the right people to work with that will keep my businesses running smoothly and allow me the free time that I need. People like you."

Audrey appreciated how open Troy was about the demands of his life. It was interesting to hear that apparently all the money in the world couldn't solve every problem. "Thank you. If you have the time, we'd love to come by."

"Can you meet me here tomorrow at six? I'll be coming from another appointment, and having the date set with you means I can't be late, right?"

"We'll see you tomorrow."

"It's a date, then." Troy squeezed her shoulder. "How late can your babysitter stay? I want to show you my theater room. We could watch a movie together?"

Audrey looked up into Troy's dark brown eyes. His expression was almost boyish in the eagerness and openness of his face as he invited her into his home and his life.

"I told her I'd be there before midnight, so I think we still have time." Audrey laughed inwardly at herself. It was almost like she was a teenager with a curfew. Mostly she was just realistic and knew that if she stayed up all night, she wouldn't have any energy or patience with the girls tomorrow.

"Okay, I can have you back by eleven thirty, so you can get plenty of beauty rest."

"Beauty rest? What's that? My sleep is more like a zombie apocalypse."

Troy laughed, and Audrey joined him. He looked at her with appreciation in his eyes. "Let's walk around a bit more. I just can't resist this time of night."

Audrey checked her watch. It was already after nine, and the sun was almost gone. "A few more minutes and the lightning bugs will be out."

Troy grinned and tugged on her hand. "Let's hurry, then. I'll take you to the best spot to see them."

Audrey followed him, walking quickly to keep up with his long strides. He led her along a winding path to the edge of the lawn, where the trees stood like sentinels guarding the forest beyond. He put his arm around her, and Audrey loved the way that she suddenly felt so safe next to him. "How far does your property go?"

"I have about thirty acres. Most of it is untamed forest, except for the ten acres the house sits on." Troy motioned to the property and peered into the trees. "Look, they're already starting."

Audrey looked, but then she turned back to Troy, studying his face carefully. The laugh lines around his eyes were apparent, and he looked relaxed, different than he often was at work. The strain and expectations of his business probably took a bigger toll on him than he realized. Hesitantly, Audrey thought back to how she'd wondered what it would be like to live in Troy's life. Would it always be stressful and busy as he tried to keep up with his next project? Her gaze trailed back to the flickers of light as lightning bugs rose and fell along the tree line.

"Audrey, thanks for sharing this night with me. It's one of the best I've had in a long time." Troy faced her, his eyes softening.

Troy touched her cheek, tilting her head upwards. His other hand rested on the small of her back, pulling her ever closer to him. The crickets chirped and the frogs croaked, as if they were miles away from civilization and it was just the two of them in the middle of the Tennessee woods. Audrey could see the outline of Troy's mansion in the distance, the canned lights shining around the covered patio.

Troy held her and he studied her face. He leaned closer and then hesitated. Audrey lifted up on her tiptoes and closed the distance between them. Her lips brushed his, and suddenly the lightning bugs were inside her, lighting up her heart, swirling around her middle, and pushing her closer to Troy. She reached her arms around his neck, and he kissed her again, softly, moving from one corner of her mouth to the other. She'd never been kissed like this before. A flame of desire engulfed the lightning bugs, and Audrey returned the kiss, hungry for the sparkling energy transferred between them.

Troy stiffened and leaned back. "I'm sorry, I shouldn't have done that." He moved to step away, but Audrey kept her arms around his neck and stumbled into him.

"Wait, Troy, wait."

He stopped moving, returned his hands to her waist, and looked in her eyes. "I don't want you to think that I expect anything. I just couldn't resist kissing you."

Audrey smiled. "Who said you were the one kissing me?" she teased, and leaned forward, brushing her lips against his again. "It's been so long since I've been this close to a man."

Troy licked his lips. "Audrey, I respect you enough to tell you that we'd better start walking back to the house."

Audrey nodded. "I agree with what you said earlier. This is one of the best nights I've had in a long time."

Troy smiled and took her hand as they made their way back to the house by the light of the fireflies blinking in the darkness. They talked softly to one another, and Audrey felt the connection to him deepen. What had started with a Frisbee flying off course was turning into something wonderful and possibly quite dangerous for her heart.

Chapter 9

Saturday flew by for Audrey and the girls. She kept them busy all morning cleaning bathrooms and tidying up the house with the promise of fishing time with Troy later. It was still hard to believe that someone like him was interested in someone like her. She could almost hear LuAnne's voice in her head disagreeing with that thought: "You're as good as you think you are. Money and perceived success don't matter. What matters is what's in the heart."

Audrey did her best to concentrate on the conversation that she and Troy had shared, the parts where she didn't worry about his success or money and how different her life was from his. It wasn't hard to keep thinking about Troy, because the night before had felt like a fairy-tale dream.

By the time Audrey and her girls arrived at Troy's mansion that evening, the excitement in their car was palpable. Katie's eyes bugged out when she saw the size of Troy's home. "It looks like a hotel, Mom!" She rolled down her window, craning her neck to see better.

Audrey parked in the massive driveway, her nerves alight with anticipation and pleasant memories of the time she'd spent with Troy. They approached the front door, Lizzie holding one hand and Katie holding the other. Before Audrey could knock, the door swung open, and they were greeted by a woman in her fifties wearing a crisp uniform. "Welcome, my name is Joyce. Mr. Jackson hasn't made it home yet," she said. "He asked that I show you inside and get you some refreshment while you wait."

Audrey felt a pang of disappointment, but she hid it well with a broad smile. "Thank you, that'll be very nice."

She followed Joyce through the large foyer, pausing once to admire a lovely statue of a woman holding a bird in her outstretched hand.

"Mommy, what is that statue for?" Lizzie asked.

"I'm not sure, but it's lovely, isn't it?" Audrey replied.

Lizzie nodded, reaching her fingertips toward the bird.

"Don't touch it!" Katie commanded before Audrey had a chance to say the same thing to Lizzie.

"Remember to look with your eyes," Audrey said.

Joyce waited a few paces down the hall for them to follow. The high ceilings of the entryway made their voices echo, and Lizzie giggled. They continued past the dining room and into a room that looked somewhat different from the rest of the house. It was still gorgeous, and exquisitely decorated, but the feeling in this room was more comfortable. There was a matching set of gray couches dotted with turquoise throw pillows. A bright yellow and white rug lay in front of the couches on the dark wood floor. A breakfast nook was built into a bay window on one end of the room, and the table was set with a pitcher of lemonade, glasses, a tray with cut-up vegetables, and another tray with cheese and crackers.

"Make yourself at home," Joyce said. "Mr. Jackson will be with you as soon as he can."

After the maid left, Audrey's phone pinged with an incoming text. She swiped the screen and smiled when she saw Troy's name.

Sorry to keep you waiting. Late and now hung up in traffic.

Audrey tapped out a reply: **We're here and looking forward to seeing you soon.**

"Now don't overdo it on the cheese and crackers, girls," Audrey said. She sat next to them and nibbled on cucumbers dipped in delicious balsamic vinaigrette with a hint of lemon. After about fifteen minutes, Audrey stood and wiped her hands on a napkin "I'm just going to walk around this room; if you girls would like to do the same, please remember your manners."

"I thought we were going fishing." Katie stacked two slices of cheese on top of a cracker and popped the whole thing in her mouth.

"We are, but Troy got stuck in traffic."

"So we're at his house and he's not coming?" Katie asked.

"He'll be here soon." Audrey hoped those words were true. She could already see her own disappointment mirrored on Katie's face. Lizzie was still munching through crackers and cheese happily, but that mood probably wouldn't last long.

A few minutes later, the maid returned, carrying a silver tray filled with food. She set it down on the round table next to the breakfast nook. The tray had three kinds of pasta and three different bowls of sauces.

"Bowtie, penne, and fettuccine pasta," Joyce said, pointing to the multicolored serving bowls, "with a choice of marinara sauce, alfredo, or sausage and cheese. Mr. Jackson asked that I begin serving you because he doesn't want the kids to get too hungry."

Audrey's shoulders slumped. "Okay, did he say when he thought he would make it?"

The maid smiled. "If all goes well, he should be here within the next half hour."

Audrey wrinkled her nose. That would mean Troy would be over an hour late. She tried to be understanding of his situation because the traffic around Nashville was usually a mess, but she'd been looking forward to this evening, wanting everything to go just right for the girls to spend time with Troy. Also, it was a bit awkward waiting in Troy's mansion, being served by his maid while he wasn't there. Audrey wondered why Troy hadn't just called her earlier. He could've told her he was running late, and she would've stayed at home with the girls.

"Mommy, can we eat now?" Lizzie brought Audrey's attention back to the meal.

Audrey decided to shelve her worry and frustration over Troy's tardiness. "Yes, everything looks delicious."

The girls ate happily, almost as if they were in a fancy restaurant, and Audrey did her best to keep her spirits up. Finally, at 7:45, Troy walked in the room.

"I apologize for being so late." He sighed. "I didn't want it to turn out this way." He stepped up to Audrey, took her hand, and lifted it to his cheek. "Can you forgive me?"

Audrey's heart melted in her chest at the same time her brain was bringing to her attention the fact that her date was nearly two hours late. Troy looked a bit harried, and his eyes searched hers with hopeful uncertainty.

"Of course we'll forgive you. You fed us, after all." Audrey motioned to the dishes on the table and pointed out Katie and Lizzie looking at books on one of his sofas. Joyce had brought out some activities for them after the meal. "What about you? You must be starving."

Troy unbuttoned the top button of his light green dress shirt. He sat down across from Audrey. "I am hungry. Do you mind if I eat, and then we can head out to the pond?"

Audrey glanced at her daughters, hoping that they would stay in a good mood. The later it got, the less predictable Lizzie might become.

Troy followed her gaze. "We could bring dessert out now."

"Go ahead and eat. They're being good right now, and if they start acting up, I'll tell them dessert is coming."

Troy relaxed visibly and picked up a fork, diving into the meal like a man on a mission. Audrey hid her smile, deciding not to worry about what had already happened.

"You don't know how much it means to me that I can relax here with you and eat my supper, even though you should be really angry at me right now for being so late."

Audrey shook her head. "Anger doesn't solve anything, but I should admit that if you hadn't fed us, I might not be smiling right now."

Troy chuckled and he motioned to his maid. "I think we're about ready for dessert now."

She nodded and walked quickly back to the kitchen.

Troy finished his meal, wiped his mouth with a napkin, and sat up straight. "Hey girls, how would you like some of my cook's famous chocolate turtle brownies and ice cream?"

Both the girls perked up, stood from the sofa, and hurried over to the table. "I want ice cream, but I don't want a turtle," Lizzie said.

Troy laughed loudly enough that Katie jumped back. "That is the cutest thing. You must get that from your mother." He turned and winked at Audrey.

"Lizzie, a turtle brownie doesn't have a turtle on it; it has caramel and pecans," Audrey explained. "The shape of it sort of reminds people of a turtle."

Lizzie looked at Troy and her mother and wrinkled her nose. Katie leaned toward the table. "Are you really rich or something?"

"Katie, that's not appropriate." Audrey touched her arm, smiling to soften the reprimand.

"That's okay, she's just curious. I was curious just like you when I was your age." Troy smiled. "I guess some people would say I'm pretty rich. But I found that money isn't the thing that makes me happy. Once I started concentrating more on people, that's when I got really successful."

He talked to Katie, but Audrey felt that the answer was also for her. She felt a little nudge from the cryptic side of her brain, reminding her to ask Troy about his past. The way he spoke indicated that he hadn't always lived the way he wanted to.

The maid came out carrying another silver tray full of beautiful glass bowls filled with dessert that look like they came out of a food magazine. The girls scooted onto the bench beside Audrey and picked up long dessert spoons with eagerness.

"It looks almost too pretty to eat," Audrey said.

"It doesn't look like turtles at all, Mom," Lizzie said around a mouthful of fudgy brownie. She licked a drip of ice cream from the corner of her mouth. Troy chuckled again. Katie took small bites, ever aware of Troy's attention.

"I heard that there are some girls who might want to go fishing now," Troy said.

"Me! I do," Lizzie said.

Troy turned to Katie. "How about you? You look like you might be a natural at casting."

Katie smiled. "Really?"

Troy nodded. "I guess we'll just have to test it out and see."

"Do we have to help with the dishes first?" Katie asked.

Audrey thought Troy would burst into laughter again. Instead his eyes softened, and he looked at Lizzie, Katie, and then Audrey. "This is my treat tonight. You don't have to lift a finger if you don't want to. My staff will take care of everything."

"Wow, I wish we had a maid." Katie seemed to appreciate the surroundings now that she understood the perks that came with a mansion like Troy's.

Troy stood. "I'll go change and be right back."

When Troy reappeared a few minutes later, he was more casual than Audrey had ever seen him before. Wearing khaki shorts and a T-shirt, he looked even younger, and Audrey was reminded just how young he was. Two years younger than her, and already a billionaire.

They headed out to the pond, the girls skipping ahead while Troy and Audrey held hands and walked along the beautifully manicured path. All of the fishing gear was waiting in the gazebo, and there was a table with more refreshments, iced tea, and sparkling cider. There was a pathway lined with gravel leading down to the edge of the pond.

"You thought of everything for tonight. This is wonderful." Audrey picked up a glass of iced tea and took a sip

"Everything but how to stop time and give me a few extra hours. Thanks again for being such a good sport when I was late." Troy turned to the girls. "Okay, who wants to cast in first?"

Troy was a natural with Katie and Lizzie. Within a few minutes, Katie was totally at ease as she held her fishing pole, slowly reeling in the line. Troy helped each girl cast out, and then he cast with his own fishing pole and set it by the side of the bank in a bright red metal pole rest. Then he picked up one more pole and handed it to Audrey. "Cast over to the left. I think you might have good luck there."

"I don't think I've done this for nearly ten years. I don't want to put somebody's eye out." Audrey gripped the pole, trying to remember her own father teaching her to fish.

"I'll give you a few pointers." Troy stood behind her, wrapping his arms around her. He placed each hand over hers, showing her how to correctly hold the fishing pole as she pulled it back. "You press this lever as you pull back and cast out across the water." The bit of scruff on Troy's cheek was scratchy against Audrey's face as he bent his head next to hers while giving her instruction. "Now you try it."

Audrey bit her lip, pulled her hand back, and flicked the fishing rod forward. The pole jerked, and the line jogged out a few yards, plopping in the water. Audrey laughed at herself and heard Troy chuckling behind her.

"Not bad for once in a decade. Let's try it again."

Audrey didn't mind when Troy put his arms around her again and helped her cast a beautiful line into the pond. A few minutes later, Katie squealed excitedly as her pole jerked, and Troy rushed over to help her reel in a fish. Lizzie screamed when the fish flopped out of the water and missed the net that Troy was holding. Audrey captured several fun pictures of Troy with the girls. They shared lots of laughter, and Audrey wished the night didn't have to end. The sun turned the sky orange as it dipped behind the trees, casting a glow across the pond.

By the time they packed it in for the night, Lizzie was asleep in Troy's arms. He carried her to the car, tucking her in gently. He patted Katie on the shoulder. "I knew you were a natural. You did great tonight."

Katie beamed up at him with a smile that made Audrey's heart thrum with hope. Her little girl, always so serious, needed someone in her life to bring out the playful side.

Troy opened Audrey's door for her, but pulled her into a hug before she could climb inside. "When can I see you again? And I don't mean at the office."

Everything about tonight had been like a dream. Being waited on, the admiration in Troy's eyes, the easy way he had with her daughters, and the obvious love he had for everyone he interacted with. "Hopefully soon."

"Do you think you might like to come to church with me tomorrow?"

Audrey shook her head. "No, I think the girls will be pretty tuckered out after the day we've had."

If Troy was disappointed, he hid it well. "I'll let you go, but only if you promise that I can take you out on another date and I'll be early this time."

"I guess I could agree to that."

Troy held her for a moment, and then brushed a quick kiss across her lips. "Good night, Audrey. Sweet dreams."

"Thank you. Good night." Audrey got in her car and waved as she pulled away from the dreamlike mansion. As she drove home, Katie chattered about all the wonderful things she noticed in Troy's home and wondered aloud just how rich he might be. Once Audrey had tucked both her girls into bed for the night, she took a moment to remember all the looks, touches, and smiles Troy had given her that night. He told her to have sweet dreams, but she wasn't sure how her dreams could be any better than tonight.

Chapter 10

The following week was a blur for Troy. Every time he tried to carve out minutes to talk to Audrey, it seemed like they were interrupted. On Friday, he cleared some time in his schedule for the following Monday to take Audrey to lunch. He was just about to call her and ask if she was available when she stopped by his office, knocking on the open doorframe.

"Hey, Troy, do you have a minute?"

Troy grinned and set his phone down. "For you, I have two. Come in and close the door."

Audrey pulled the door closed as Troy walked around his desk toward her. She turned and smiled when she saw how close he was to her. "I just had one quick question. I know you're busy."

Troy put his arms around Audrey and pulled her to him. "The chiropractor told me I should get up from my desk every half hour and walk around. I'm just following doctor's orders." He bent and kissed her cheek. "Now, what can I do for you?"

Audrey pulled his head toward hers and kissed him on the mouth. Troy smiled against her kiss, liking the way that she reached up on her tiptoes to kiss him again. Audrey put her hand on his cheek. "I promise I didn't come in here just to kiss you."

"And why is that?"

"Because I wanted to come in for no reason at all, but …" She looked down at the floor, biting her lip.

Troy put his finger under her chin and tipped her head back so he could look into her beautiful blue eyes. "I've been missing you all week, but Rachel is a strict ruler over my schedule." He shook his head. "I should have tried harder. I need to see you, Audrey. I was just about to call and ask you if you could go to lunch with me on Monday."

Audrey's face broke into a wide smile. "I'd love to. What did you have in mind?"

"There's this great little Mexican place. It's not far from the Grand Ole Opry, and I was thinking if you haven't taken a tour yet, we could go together."

"Really? I've wanted to take a tour ever since we moved here." Audrey bounced up on her toes and kissed him quickly.

"Well, how about we tour the Ryman Auditorium—that's what the locals called it long before it was called the Grand Ole Opry—and then grab lunch on Monday?" Troy tucked a strand of red hair behind her ear.

"That sounds wonderful."

Troy leaned down and kissed her gently, savoring the way her mouth felt against his. "Now, what was it you needed?"

Audrey smiled. "I need you … to approve a few changes that Felicia and I have made to what will be track six on her debut record."

Troy hesitated, loving the way that Audrey had paused after saying, "I need you." He took her hand and tugged her toward the chair in front of his desk. He walked slowly around his desk, sitting down and picking up a pen. "I have a few minutes now. Tell me what you'd like to do."

Audrey grinned and leaned forward. As she spoke, Troy watched her eyes sparkle with light and the way her perfect lips tilted upward as she described the music they were working on. He would have to rearrange his schedule again, because lunch on Monday wasn't enough time with the vivacious woman in front of him.

On Monday, Audrey dressed carefully in white capris and a gauzy lavender blouse. She pulled her hair back in a loose braid and slipped on her favorite silver wedge sandals. She had enjoyed a leisurely morning with the girls, and then LuAnne had stopped by to take them all to the pool so Audrey could go into work. She didn't have any appointments until after lunch, and her skin tingled with anticipation of spending time with Troy. She had treasured every touch and passing glance he'd given her last week, but it wasn't enough for either of them.

When she arrived at Arise Music, Rachel stood, and her hands fluttered at her side. "Oh, Audrey, I'm afraid I have some bad news. Troy won't be able to make it for lunch today. He wanted me to tell you that he'll call as soon as he can, but he had an urgent meeting on the other side of the city."

Audrey couldn't keep the disappointment from tugging at her smile. She'd been looking forward to this date more than she probably should have. "Oh. Thanks for telling me."

Rachel wrung her hands. "Oh, he was so upset about having to cancel. He wants to reschedule as soon as possible. Troy really does try hard to keep his appointments."

"Thanks, Rachel. I'll just use the extra time to prepare for my session with Jake today."

Audrey walked to the studio and took a few minutes to pull out her notes, but she couldn't concentrate. It was hard to believe that Troy couldn't even take a moment to text her about the cancellation, but Audrey tried not to dwell on that.

Fifteen minutes later, Audrey caught a whiff of something spicy and delicious, and her stomach reminded her that she would need to figure out what to eat for lunch.

"Here's lunch, courtesy of Troy and Taco Mamacita," Rachel said as she handed Audrey a takeout box. "You're a very lucky gal, ya know."

Audrey nodded. "I'm beginning to think so." She took the box and opened the aromatic sampling of tacos, beans, and seasoned rice. Relief curled around the edges of her hunger as she took the first bite, because Troy hadn't forgotten her. She could appreciate that he really was busy and doing his best to juggle life. Audrey settled into her chair and ate one of the most delicious Mexican meals she'd had in a long time. Although she'd really been looking forward to touring the Ryman Auditorium and learning about the birthplace of country music at the Grand Ole Opry, Audrey consoled herself by tasting each bite of Troy's thoughtfulness. He didn't have to order takeout for her, but he had because he hadn't wanted her to go hungry. Audrey took another bite and smiled. At least they already had a good idea for the next date.

Troy was pulled in every direction the next few days: putting out fires, attending recording appointments, approving changes in upcoming records. Audrey had worked for a few hours on Wednesday, and he hadn't even been able to see her. He still regretted having to cancel Monday's lunch, and what made it worse was that by the time he'd caught up with everything and come up for air, it had been almost two weeks since their last date. When he'd called Audrey to apologize, she'd assured him that she was busy herself, putting in several extra coaching sessions with Felicia Perry and Jake Mendez and spending lots of time with her girls during the summer break.

By Thursday, Troy couldn't wait another minute. He finished a phone call with one of his studio techs and called Audrey, who was at home for the day. "Audrey, I have to see you. How about tonight?"

"Well, it's kind of short notice for me to find a babysitter, but I can try."

Troy groaned. "I have to see you. I'm sorry I had to cancel last time."

"I understand," Audrey said. But her voice said more than just words. It was laced with disappointment, and she sounded tired.

Troy decided to be bold. "I'm coming by after work, and I'll bring takeout. We can hang out at your place, and you won't have to get a sitter."

There was a pause. Audrey cleared her throat. "Actually, I think that's a good idea. What time do you think you can get here?"

"I will be there by six-thirty, and if anybody needs me in the office when it's time for me to leave, I'll pull the fire alarm."

Audrey laughed. "Don't do anything drastic. Just try your best and we'll be here."

Troy smiled. "I can't wait to see you."

After he hung up, Troy checked the agenda that Rachel had updated for him in the last hour. He made a few phone calls, keeping the small talk to a minimum and working through his list as if it were a chore chart.

At five thirty, Mike walked into his office and shut the door. "Hey, you busy?"

Troy glanced pointedly at the clock and said, "I have ten minutes and I'm out of here."

"Okay, I can do ten." Mike sat down and leaned forward, putting his forearms on his knees.

Troy groaned. "I hate that stance; you remind me of my old basketball coach. What did I do wrong now?"

Mike grinned. "Nothing yet, but I am worried. I thought I told you to stay away from Audrey Blair."

Troy bristled, sitting up straight in his chair. "And I told you that I'm responsible and I should've told you to mind your own business, but I'm telling you now."

Mike shook his head, his grin flattening into a straight line. "You know I'm always looking out for you, Troy. Audrey is doing an excellent job, and you getting serious with her is a recipe for trouble."

"Who said I was getting serious?" Troy asked.

"I did. I know you, and I can see it all over your face. You've been acting different, too. In a good way, but still …"

"Mike, when are you going to trust me? I'm not going to hurt Audrey. I care about her a lot, and we get along great."

Mike rested his chin in his hand. "Oh, so you've told her about the other Troy?"

Troy flinched. Mike wasn't going to let him off the hook, but Troy wasn't serious with Audrey yet. At least, he wasn't serious enough about her to share those dark parts of his past that were no longer welcome in his life. "That's a pretty heavy topic to delve into when you've only known someone a few weeks. I'll tell her when I'm ready, not before."

Mike didn't say anything for five seconds, because Troy was counting them as the minute hand ticked closer to six o'clock. Mike took his hand from underneath his chin, clenched it into a fist, and pounded his palm. "All I know is you've waited a long time, and I do trust you. But you need to tell her soon. The media may seem like they've taken a break from you, but they're like wolves. If they even catch a whiff of something that might make a good story, they'll start chewing until they draw blood."

Troy felt Mike's words. The warning stepped up his spine and sent a cold chill across his shoulders. The last thing he wanted to do was hurt Audrey. But if he told her now … he shook his head. "I can't tell her yet, Mike. I know it doesn't make sense to you." He put a hand over his heart and tapped two fingers. "But in here, I know it's not right to tell her."

Mike nodded and stood as he straightened his tie. "Let me know if you need any help with that."

"I will."

Mike pulled his bottom lip through his teeth. "No hard feelings?"

Troy shook his head. "We're good, as usual, Bulldog."

Mike chuckled at the nickname Troy called him when he was hanging on to an idea like a dog on a bone. Then his brow furrowed. "I almost forgot, Felicia was asking a few questions. She said she'd been approached by an agent who is really big on musicians going indie."

"Well, she's already signed a contract." Troy stood and looked out the window toward Music Row. "Besides, if he's really an agent, he wouldn't be urging her to go indie, because she wouldn't need an agent. I hope you told her that."

"I did. Seems he was trying to get some information out of her, is all I can guess. I told her to be careful and set up a meeting for her to meet with legal to go over her contract, just as a refresher."

Troy looked down at his feet, letting out a slow breath. It wouldn't be the first time that he'd had troubles with a brand-new musician navigating the do's and don'ts of working with the production company. He'd already paid Felicia a sizable advance on her first record, and the girl had a lot of talent. The last thing he wanted was to lose his investments, as well as her potential career. "Thanks for staying on top of things, Mike. I know you'll help her get through any questions, but definitely tell her to set up an appointment with me if she needs to."

"Will do. Have a good night."

Mike left and Troy allowed himself sixty seconds to take a few notes and decompress after the emotionally taxing conversation. Then he switched off his computer and headed out the door. He had to take a few back roads after he picked up Chinese food from his favorite takeout place, but he pulled into Audrey's driveway at six twenty-nine. He couldn't help smiling as he jumped out of his car, lifting the bag of food and heading for the door. He knocked, and Katie opened the door.

"Hi, Katie. How are you doing?"

"Hi, Troy. Come in if you want," she mumbled. She didn't look happy to see him. Troy remembered Audrey saying something about Katie going through some moods, so he chose to ignore it.

Troy stepped across the threshold and was met by a growl. He jumped back, startled by Duke, who must've been standing in the shadow of the door. "Hey, Duke." He held out one hand in front of Duke, but the dog eyed the sack of food. Troy lifted it higher. "Guess I better get this in the kitchen before Duke takes his share, right?"

Katie nodded. "Duke, no. Stay." She held out her hand, pushing against Duke's nose until the dog backed up two steps. Troy was again impressed by how obedient the German Shepherd was, even with a sack full of aromatic Chinese food tempting him.

"Next time you'll have to remember to bring the dog a treat as well." Audrey came around the corner, her face brightening into a beautiful smile. "You made it."

Troy held out the bag of food. "Just barely. I'd better let you take this before Duke helps himself."

Audrey peered around Troy, making eye contact with Duke. "Come on back to your room and I'll feed you, Duke."

Troy watched as Audrey walked into the kitchen with Duke trotting obediently behind her. She showed the dog into the mud room and served him up a scoop of dog food. She scratched behind his ears. "Good boy."

When Audrey reentered the kitchen, Troy pulled her into a hug. "I've missed you. Thanks for letting me come over."

Audrey wrapped her arms around his waist. "I'm glad you invited yourself. I've missed you too."

Troy leaned down and pecked her on the cheek. Audrey smiled and turned slowly out of his arms. "Girls, you ready to eat?"

Katie and Lizzie hurried into the kitchen and sat on two of the three barstools at the counter. Audrey started pulling out cartons of food and passing them around to the girls. She glanced at Troy. "We'll sit at the table, if you don't mind."

"That sounds great." Troy's stomach grumbled as he dished up his own plate of food. Before he lifted his fork, he looked around, noticing that the girls were already eating and Audrey was munching on a bite. He didn't want to make her uncomfortable, but he just couldn't eat without thanking God for his food. So he bowed his head and whispered a silent prayer. When he lifted his head, Audrey was studying him, one eyebrow arched. Troy smiled and shrugged. "Habit," he said.

Audrey nodded and sat down. "I wouldn't have minded if you wanted to offer a prayer."

"I don't want to make you feel uncomfortable," Troy replied.

"Then don't. You're the owner of a Christian record company. I get that God is a big part of your life, and I'm okay with that."

Troy pulled his fork through the rice on his plate. "Thank you. For what it's worth, I think God is a big part of your life too."

Audrey rolled her eyes, picked up her fork, and took a big bite of orange chicken. "This is good," she said in between bites.

Troy decided not to press the issue. Audrey had her past, and he didn't want to push her away. The thought brought up the conversation between him and Mike earlier. It made his stomach twist unpleasantly. Maybe there would be time to talk later that night.

Everyone had their fill of Chinese food, and the girls watched cartoons while Audrey and Troy cleaned up the kitchen. He didn't tell her that he couldn't remember the last time he'd washed dishes, or that seeing her scrubbing out the sink made her even more attractive for reasons he couldn't explain. He helped Audrey read to the girls and tucked them into bed. When she sang them a lullaby, her voice clear and beautiful and filled with so much love, Troy admitted to himself that he was falling in love with Audrey Blair. They walked down the stairs together, holding hands.

"Your voice is beautiful, Audrey." Troy looked her in the eye so she would know that he meant it.

"Thank you," Audrey replied. She stared back at him, her eyes lighting up with happiness.

After a moment, she squeezed his hand, and they continued walking down the stairs. They sat on the loveseat in her living room, chatting about work and the heat wave that was sure to come. As they talked, Troy could hear Mike's voice in his head urging him to tell Audrey about his past. But there wasn't any kind of an opening in their conversation for him to attempt to delve into the dark shadows of his history.

Audrey was so grateful to be sitting next to Troy in her living room, even though at the moment he seemed miles away from her. She nudged him with her foot. "It seems like you have a lot on your mind tonight." She traced her fingers along his hand.

Troy turned his hand with the palm facing up and interlaced his fingers with hers. "I was just thinking how thankful I am for how patient you've been with me and how busy my schedule's been. I hope you don't think you're an afterthought. All I can think about is you." He chuckled.

Audrey leaned into his shoulder, and he lifted his arm and pulled her in closer. "I've had a few thoughts, worried a little, but I see how hard you work. I'm trying to understand and be patient."

"But my time is yours tonight," Troy said. "What would you like to do?"

Audrey leaned her head back against the couch and breathed out slowly. "Would you ... would you hold me? Sometimes I just want to be held."

Troy put his arm around her, and she snuggled in closer. After a few minutes, she could feel his heart thumping against her cheek.

Troy cleared his throat. "I—uh, I'm not sure this is the best idea for me."

Audrey lifted her head, looking him in the eyes. "Why?"

"Because I'm more than a little attracted to you." He wiped his brow with his other hand. "I made a commitment to myself a long time ago that I'm saving myself for marriage, and I've done everything I can to keep that."

She straightened. "Wow, that's rare and very admirable."

He didn't smile. "It's the right thing to do."

"I can honor that. I didn't mean to tempt you." Audrey tried to tamp down the slow burn of attraction that she had for Troy as she sat up.

He pulled her closer for a moment and then kissed the top of her head before letting her go. "There's a lot that I still need to tell you, but you know how it is with things from the past. It's never easy." Troy leaned forward, putting his hands on his knees.

"What do you mean?"

He chewed on his bottom lip for a moment and then straightened back up, looking over at her. "I mean, I haven't always been in the Christian music business. I decided to do this because I wanted to help people—to be a positive influence."

"Yes, you mentioned that before. You seem like you were born to this kind of profession, though. Your record company is so successful."

Troy shook his head. "It wasn't before. I kept my fortune growing by buying out struggling businesses and revitalizing them. Arise Music was one of those investments, but it was the first kind of investment that really meant something to me. I knew if I didn't save it, the music couldn't help save anyone else."

Audrey placed her hand on top of his, circling her thumb across his fingers. "I love that, Troy. It must feel good to make such a difference in the world."

Troy seemed uncomfortable with her praise. He swallowed, rubbed a hand across his forehead, and nodded. "It does feel better every day, but sometimes it feels like I'm running from my past. I just want to be the kind of person God knows I can be."

"Well, I think you're doing a pretty good job," Audrey said.

"But there's so much more to me than this record company." He pushed his hand through his hair and groaned. "How can I explain—"

"Mommy! Mommy, come quick!" Katie yelled from somewhere upstairs. Duke barked and bounded up the stairs as Audrey scrambled off the couch, following him. When she reached Katie's room, she flipped on the light and saw her daughter sitting up in bed with a book and a flashlight.

"Katie, are you okay?"

Troy came in the bedroom behind Audrey, breathing hard. "What happened?"

Katie turned off the flashlight and looked from Audrey to Troy and then back to Audrey again. "The shadows were scaring me."

Audrey narrowed her eyes. "Young lady, I understand that you might be scared, but you don't yell like that unless it really is an emergency. You scared me half to death."

Katie glared at Troy. "I don't like him here when I'm trying to go to sleep."

Troy stiffened next to Audrey. She reached out and grabbed his hand. "Katie, Troy is our guest tonight. He and I are talking before he has to leave. I'm going to tuck you in again, and I want you to go to sleep, please."

Troy cleared his throat. "I'm sorry I made it hard for you to sleep, Katie. I'll be leaving in five minutes."

Audrey's lungs constricted, and she struggled to keep her breathing normal as frustration rose up. He'd been about to tell her something important, before Katie had cried wolf. She pasted a smile on her face, leaning down to kiss Katie's cheek as she tucked her in the bed. Audrey hummed a snippet of a lullaby as she brushed Katie's hair back from her face with her fingertips. "Good night, Katie. I love you very much."

Audrey and Troy didn't speak again until they had reached the bottom of the stairs.

"I guess I'd better be going," Troy said.

Audrey's shoulders slumped. "I wish you didn't have to, but it's probably a good idea." The moment for confiding in each other had passed, and there wasn't anything Audrey could do to recall it. Instead she reached out and hugged Troy. "Thank you for coming. I hope I'll get another chance to get to know more about you."

Troy turned and kissed her cheek, and then kissed her on the mouth. As he pulled back, Audrey leaned forward and kissed him again. Troy chuckled. "See you tomorrow."

Audrey leaned against the open door, holding on to Troy's fingertips as he walked down her steps. She blew him a kiss and watched him climb into his Mercedes. After he'd driven off, she walked through the house and sat on the patio next to Duke. "I think I might be in a little bit of trouble, Duke. I really like Troy."

Duke licked her hand, and she scratched between his ears. She sat there for a few minutes more and then climbed the stairs stealthily to check on Katie. Her daughter was fast asleep, her performance already forgotten. Audrey would have to figure out how to talk to her daughters about the possibility of their mommy dating another man. Lizzie wouldn't have a problem with it, but she was afraid of what else Katie might try to do.

Audrey got ready for bed much earlier than she'd expected, but it was probably a good idea. There was a lot to do in the few days left before the Fourth of July celebrations began. She pulled back her light cotton sheets and hesitated before climbing into bed. For most of her life, Audrey had knelt at her bedside and prayed to God each night before going to sleep. Hearing Troy talk tonight had stirred up a reminder in her soul. Memories of the many times she'd prayed to God and felt He was listening tugged at the black curtain she'd drawn over that part of her heart. Audrey got into bed, repositioning her pillow a few times. "I just want Katie to understand that I'll always love her," Audrey whispered. She closed her eyes, ignoring the similarity of her whispered words to a prayer.

Chapter 11

Audrey didn't get to see much of Troy over the next couple days, but on Friday he called her into his office. When Audrey walked past Rachel's desk, the secretary smiled brightly "I've never seen him like this before. Whatever you're doing, keep on doing it."

Audrey blushed. "I'm not doing anything. We've only been on a few dates."

Rachel nodded. "I know, I mean whatever you're doing to his heart. He's like a little kid in a candy shop in there. Wait 'til you find out."

"Okay?" Audrey was half tempted to ask Rachel for more details, but the secretary looked genuinely happy for whatever Troy was about to tell her in his office. Audrey hurried inside, closing the door behind her.

Troy jumped up from his desk. "Audrey, it's so good to see you." He walked across the room and hugged her, and then he pulled back and kissed her on the mouth with an intensity that sent currents of happiness clear down through Audrey's toes.

"Troy, what's going on?" Audrey giggled as Troy nuzzled her neck.

"Please say you'll celebrate the Fourth of July with me? You and your girls, I mean." Troy watched her face, his eyes eager with whatever he had planned.

Audrey grinned. "Will there be sparklers? You know it's not the Fourth of July without sparklers."

"Sparklers, yes. Multicolored sparklers, long-burning sparklers, LED sparklers." Troy ticked off an imaginary list on his fingers. "Will you come to my house for a barbecue and fireworks?"

Audrey could only imagine what kind of Fourth of July celebration Troy Jackson would put on at his mansion. "We wouldn't miss it. Would you like us to bring anything?"

Troy shook his head. "This isn't a potluck. It's a party, but you are the only ones invited. I hope you don't mind."

Audrey had just been anticipating how she might deal with all the people clamoring for Troy's attention when his words registered. "You mean, this isn't for your company? Just us?"

Troy grinned. "Party of four at the Jackson residence on the Fourth. Has a nice ring to it, doesn't it?"

"It does."

"I wanted to invite Duke too, but I'm guessing he won't like the kind of fireworks we'll have that night."

Audrey nodded. "Duke will be much happier at home, but I'll send him your regards."

"Does six o'clock sound okay?"

"Yes, that'll be perfect."

"Good. I'm going out of town, but I'll be back late the night of the third. I wanted to make sure and ask you before I had to leave." He leaned in and pecked her cheek. "There never seems to be enough hours in the day to get enough of you, Audrey Blair."

Audrey put her arms around his neck and pressed her lips along his jawline. He was clean-shaven and a hint of his woodsy aftershave tickled her nose. She hesitated by his ear and whispered, "I feel the same way."

Troy kissed her then, his hands on the small of her back, pulling her close. And then, as if something snapped in him, he stopped, pulled back, and released her. "Sorry," he murmured.

"Troy, you don't have to apologize for wanting to kiss me," Audrey said. She placed her hand on his cheek.

He turned his head and kissed her palm. "Okay, just don't let Mike catch us in here, or he'll have my hide."

"Aren't you the boss?" Audrey raised her eyebrows.

"Most of the time." Troy tilted his head. "But Mike likes to keep me in line, especially when it has something to do with his new vocal coach."

"Okay, I'll get back to work, then." Audrey pulled herself away from the magnetic energy pulsing off Troy.

"Thanks, Audrey. You're making a difference around here. I hope you know that."

"I'm starting to feel that way. I really enjoyed working with Felicia and Jake."

"Good, because if Mike has his way, he'll be adding a few more to your list."

"I'll be ready." Audrey walked to the door, put her hand on the doorknob, and turned back to Troy. "See you on the Fourth."

"I'm starting the countdown now to the fireworks show." Troy tapped his phone screen, and Audrey believed that he actually was starting a countdown. She left his office grinning like a schoolgirl.

"See, I knew you'd be smiling. You two are so cute together," Rachel gushed.

Audrey straightened, her smile faltering. Rachel had never really seen them together—at least, Audrey didn't think so, unless she had some sort of video surveillance set up in Troy's office.

"I just picture you two in my mind's eye whenever Troy sets something up for you," Rachel continued. "You have a wonderful day now."

"Thank you. I will." Audrey felt a bit flustered under Rachel's enthusiastic scrutiny. It was only after she'd walked away that she realized she hadn't wished her a good day. Audrey thought about Troy's worry over Mike Cheatham. She supposed that not everyone at Arise Studios would be as excited as Rachel Graham to see her dating the owner. She shrugged and scheduled the fireworks invite on her calendar. She couldn't stop smiling for the rest of the day.

Troy found it hard to concentrate over the next few days; he wanted to be with Audrey and get to know her girls better. He really did have a countdown on his phone, and every time he was in another boring meeting, he checked the counter, marking the hours until he could see her again. He'd enlisted Rachel to help line up a party that wouldn't easily be forgotten.

He planned to stop by and visit his parents in the morning and early afternoon, leaving him plenty of time to get things ready for the evening celebration with Audrey.

A few times, his mind wandered to the conversation he'd almost had with Audrey at her house. He'd been a breath away from telling her about his past when Katie had started screaming. He still couldn't decide if the little girl had saved him or caused more trouble. Every time he ran into Mike at the office, he seemed to ask the question with his eyes: *Have you told her yet?* Troy didn't even have to shake his head; his open face revealed the truth to Mike. He would tell her after the Fourth of July. They could enjoy that evening, get to know one another better, and then he would plan a date where they could share a conversation in private. He even called Rachel and asked her to make room in his schedule for a lunch date on Thursday. That was the next day Audrey would be in the office after the holiday. He vowed that he wouldn't let another day pass without telling her the truth.

Chapter 12

On Monday, July third, Audrey headed into Nashville early, excited for her next appointment with Felicia Perry. The music they were working on for her debut record was going well, and Felicia's eagerness to learn made each session great. They'd arranged to squeeze in an extra session before the holiday, and Audrey was happy to see that her coaching was making a difference.

When she arrived at Arise Music and entered the studio, Felicia was there waiting for her.

"Oh, hello. You're early. Do we need to get started earlier today?" Audrey checked her watch and mentally checked her schedule, worried that she might've forgotten.

"No, I'm here because I wanted to talk to you about something," Felicia said.

It was then that Audrey noticed Felicia twisting her hands in her lap. Her blonde hair was pulled back in a ponytail and hung straight down her back. She seemed nervous.

"That's just fine. Tell me what you need." Audrey sat down in a chair across from Felicia.

Felicia bit her lip, hesitated, and then leaned forward. "I've been really worried that maybe I made a mistake by signing with Arise."

Audrey's throat constricted and she swallowed. Was she doubting her contract because of Audrey? Maybe the sessions hadn't been going as well as Audrey thought. "But why would you think that? Everyone is so excited to have you here. I've seen some of the promotional work they have planned for your first record. It's going to be great."

"That's just it. I never thought outside of what was presented to me. I didn't think I had any other options. And now there's this guy. He's an agent, and he told me that I have a shot to hit it big."

Audrey waited a moment before answering, trying to find the words that would help this young woman. "Felicia, I don't know who this guy is or what kind of agent he is. All I know is that before today, I never heard you say a word about hitting it big. I *have* heard you say a lot about sharing the gospel message through your music. You told me you wanted to be part of uplifting people's lives." Audrey paused, gauging Felicia's reaction to her words. Her eyes widened, but she listened intently, so Audrey continued. "It's important to be sure your vision isn't getting lost in someone else's dreams."

Felicia tucked her head toward her chest. "I know. You're right. I guess I'm just scared. I've been trying to be careful with my advance because I had to quit my full-time job in order to do this."

Audrey gripped her pen, thinking through the words she needed to say. "I'm a lot older than you, but at the same time I'm not. It hasn't been that long since I was your age, staring down the possibilities the world had for me." Audrey set the pen down on a pad of paper. "Can I tell you something I've learned?"

Felicia nodded. "Of course."

"Every time I made a decision based solely on money, it turned out to be the wrong one. When I checked my gut and listened to my heart, good things happened."

"What if my gut's all twisted up inside worrying about money? What if I can't hear my heartbeat over the sound of an empty bank account?" Felicia pulled the end of her ponytail through her hands. "I come from a poor family. I've always helped support my brother. He's in college, working so hard on a degree in engineering. He says he might have to take the next semester off. I know if he stops now, he won't ever go back," Felicia said. "That's what happened to our parents."

"What kind of money is this agent offering you?" Audrey folded her arms. "And is he more than just an agent? Have things gotten personal between you two?"

Felicia's cheeks flushed. She ducked her head. "He's really good-looking. I'll admit I'm attracted to him, and he seems to be interested in me."

Audrey felt sick to her stomach as memories of how Drew had used her washed over her. "Felicia, you have to separate all that and look really hard at what you want most from your life. Take some time, research Troy. He's a good man, and he definitely doesn't need to be running a Christian music record company. He chose to do this because he felt called to it. I may not agree with everything you say about God, but I know that you couldn't have picked a better company to work with."

Tears welled up in Felicia's eyes. She stood and hugged Audrey, pulled her up from her chair. "Thank you. Thank you so much. This is just what I needed to hear." She stepped back and wiped her eyes. "'Trust in the Lord with all thine heart; and lean not unto thine own understanding.' It's one of my favorite scriptures."

Audrey knew the one. It used to be one of hers, a favorite from Bible study. Even if her relationship with God had changed, the message of the scripture still rang true. "That's probably the best advice anyone could give you."

"So, what did you mean about you and God?" Felicia asked.

"Oh, it's nothing. I got divorced a few years ago, and there's been a lot to work through. My husband cheated on me multiple times."

Felicia covered her mouth and shook her head. Then she dropped her hand, reached out and squeezed Audrey's. "I'm so sorry you had to go through that. It's obvious God is watching over you. He's watching over me too, because I just knew you were the person I needed to talk to about this. He told me so."

Audrey looked away, sniffed, and picked up her pen and pad of paper. "Well, I have just a few things to get ready before our session. In about fifteen minutes?"

Felicia nodded and hurried out the door. Audrey was grateful when the door clicked shut, because Felicia had been stepping too close to the boundaries of her faith.

Chapter 13

udrey sprayed Katie and Lizzie thoroughly with sunscreen and bug spray before heading to Troy's house on Independence Day. They drove over to Brentwood with Audrey trying to engage Katie in conversation. Her daughter was sullen and moody, because she knew they were going to Troy's house.

"Why do we have to spend our vacation at Troy's house?"

"Because he invited us and is throwing a special fireworks party just for us," Audrey replied. It was apparent that Katie wasn't okay with Audrey replacing Drew, even though Katie's father hadn't talked to her in nearly two years. Some part of her young heart still idolized the man who had hurt all of them so much, and even though Audrey hated the pain she could see in Katie's eyes, she didn't know how to help her daughter understand.

"I don't want to go." Katie folded her arms and pushed her head back against the seat.

"Well, I want to," Lizzie protested. "He's going to have sparklers. Right, Mommy?"

"He sure is. He told me he's even going to have colored sparklers. Doesn't that sound fun, Katie?" Audrey looked over at her daughter and saw the corner of her mouth twitch. "You know, when I was a little girl I loved sparklers. I would light them up and write my name in the sky as it burned. Then I would close my eyes and I could still see my name. It was one of my favorite things." Audrey looked at Katie out of the corner of her eye; her daughter was doing her best not to act interested.

"I want to do that, Mommy." Lizzie bounced her feet against the back of Audrey's seat.

Audrey smiled. "Well, this is our night. I hope that everyone will have a good attitude and remember their manners. Anyone who doesn't will have five extra chores tomorrow."

Katie frowned, but she straightened up in her seat. The girls knew that Audrey didn't make idle threats. A few minutes later they entered the gate at the Jackson mansion. Audrey pulled slowly down the drive that was lined with a dozen flags.

"Mommy, look at the flags!" Lizzie squealed.

There were two bouquets of balloons tied to either side of the entrance pillars as they approached the front door. Audrey caught Katie looking around carefully. Once again, the door swung open as they approached. Joyce motioned for them to come in. "Mr. Jackson is ready for you on the patio." She led the way through the expansive hall and opened the glass doors that were so clean Audrey would've walked right through them.

Troy had on a white short-sleeve button-up shirt and dark blue shorts. His brown eyes lit up when Audrey and the girls stepped onto the patio. He was clean-shaven, his bronze skin glistening in the sunlight. The hair on his forehead curled at the edges from the ever-present humidity.

"Happy Fourth of July, girls," Troy said. "I have a little something for you." He motioned to the beautifully laid picnic table on the patio. It sat in the shade under a large bamboo ceiling fan whirring above it. The far section of the patio was screened in completely, and Audrey thought she felt a cool rush of air from air conditioning, but she couldn't be certain. Troy came forward and kissed Audrey on the cheek. "You look beautiful."

"Thank you. You look pretty fine yourself." Audrey gripped his hand, squeezing his fingers. Audrey had on a white sundress with a turquoise beaded necklace. She'd taken extra time preparing for tonight, wanting to look her best for Troy. Her hair was pulled back in a messy bun, a few tendrils framing her face.

Troy brushed a piece of hair behind her ear. "I'm so glad you're here," he whispered. Then he straightened and called out, "Check the picnic table for your prize."

The girls scampered over to the table and picked up candy necklaces with glow sticks hanging from the middle.

"That's for the fireworks," Troy said. "You two will be the sweetest lightning bugs out there."

"Thank you!" Lizzie exclaimed.

Katie examined the necklace, and Audrey saw her try to hold back a smile. She glanced her way, and Audrey arched one eyebrow. "Thank you," Katie said quietly.

"Thank you for coming," Troy replied. "It would have been mighty lonely if it were just me and all this food."

Lizzie scanned the table that was laden with bowls and platters of food. She giggled. "You *could* probably eat all this yourself, but we'll help you."

Audrey laughed. Troy helped each of them into their seats, and they chatted for a few minutes while Joyce poured iced teas.

"Katie, has anyone ever told you that you look just like your mama?" Troy tilted his head, looking back and forth between mother and daughter.

Katie lifted her head, cautiously studying Troy. "No, not really."

And they hadn't. Katie's hair was more brown than red, and her eyes were green, but as she grew, Audrey could see more and more of herself in her daughter.

"Well, I expect if we pulled out a picture of your mama when she was nine, she would look just like you. Absolutely beautiful."

Katie smiled and ducked her head.

"She even has the same five freckles on her nose that I did when I was her age." Audrey touched the tip of Katie's nose. "Although those are multiplied by a few and then some." She tapped her own nose and both the girls laughed.

Troy leaned over, close to Audrey's face, studying her nose. "She's right. There are definitely more than five." He kissed the tip of her nose quickly. "And I love every one of them."

He lifted his eyes to hers, and Audrey felt like she was a sparkler being lit from the inside out. Troy might've been talking about her freckles, but the look in his eyes said he was talking about a whole lot more of her than just the tip of her nose. Audrey smiled. "Thank you."

Joyce brought out steaming barbecue chicken and ribs, and everyone dug in. The meat was delicious and paired with the perfectly seasoned potato salad and homemade dinner rolls. When Joyce brought out a cake, the girls cheered. It was frosted with large rosettes in red, white, and blue all along the three layers. When she cut the cake, even Katie couldn't hide her appreciation as Joyce served the slice of cake that was red, white, and blue on the inside as well.

"Well done, Joyce." Troy lifted a bite of cake to his mouth and closed his eyes as he chewed.

Audrey copied his movements as the moist cake seemed to melt on her tongue. The heat outside of their air-conditioned patio would've melted the cake; instead they lounged just outside of the stifling humidity and enjoyed every bite of their dessert.

"I think it's about time for a dip in the pool. What do you think?" Troy stood and stretched, posing the question to Katie and Lizzie.

"Yes! I'm ready," Lizzie squealed.

"Well, almost," Audrey said. "We need to get changed first."

Troy had invited everyone to bring their swimsuits because they'd have plenty of time to swim before dark. Audrey hadn't even noticed the pool on her first visit because it was on a corner of the property that they hadn't explored. She was a little nervous about wearing her swimsuit in front of Troy, but she made herself get over the nerves. Katie and Lizzie were absolutely ecstatic about the chance to swim in a private pool.

"Grab your bag, and I'll show you the pool house," Troy said.

Katie pushed back her chair and hurried over to the corner, grabbing the swim bag and hefting it over her shoulder. At least she was excited about swimming, and she'd been very well behaved during dinner.

Troy took Audrey's hand as they walked along a path lined with round paving stones. A hedge with dark green glossy leaves reached higher than Troy's head as they walked. When they turned the corner to the right, Audrey realized why she hadn't seen the pool before. It was nearly hidden, cleverly encircled by the tall hedge.

Katie gasped. "It has two slides!"

The pool was magnificent. It was shaped like a large kidney bean, one end dedicated to an area for children with the tube slide on one side and an open slide on the other. The steps were lined with red, yellow, and blue tiles, and there was a floating rope line across the water marking the spot where it dropped off from four feet, then extending to the other end of the pool. Comfortable-looking lounge chairs with umbrellas rimmed the pool. Troy tugged on her hand, leading her to the pool house, which might've been larger than some people's homes.

"This is beautiful," Audrey said. "Do you like to swim a lot?"

"I've always loved to swim. The trick is making the time to do it. I put this in a couple years ago, but it hasn't seen as much use as I'd hoped."

Audrey wondered about that for a moment. Having so much money, and basically everything at your fingertips, but still fighting the battle against time that even the poorest person had to deal with. Troy opened the door, and they walked into the pool house, complete with several spacious cupboards and his and her showers. "Wow, this is fantastic. I think I'd be out here every morning if this was in my backyard."

Troy nodded. "Most mornings that's where you'll find me when I'm in town." He motioned to the men's room. "I'll meet you out at the pool in a few minutes."

Audrey helped both girls change into a swimsuit and tucked a few loose strands of hair back into her ponytail bun. Then she changed into her green and black swimsuit, tying a swimsuit cover-up around her waist. They exited the pool house, shielding their eyes against the late evening sun. The temperature and humidity were still intense enough that Audrey removed her cover-up and splashed into the pool with the girls. The water felt cool against her hot skin, and she looked up to see Troy standing just outside the pool house finishing up a phone call. He set his cell phone inside and then walked quickly toward them with a smile.

"Sorry about that. I thought for sure I'd be faster than three girls," he teased.

Audrey admired him as he climbed into the pool, his flat stomach tensing as the water touched him. His arms were muscular and as he walked toward her, Audrey felt self-conscious for half a second until she focused on the look in his eyes. His eyes appeared lighter under the bright sun, but they weren't filled with lust; instead, Audrey felt like he was really seeing *her*.

"Once again, you look beautiful." Troy put his hands on her shoulders and moved closer. Audrey was anticipating a kiss.

Instead, she was splashed with cool water accompanied by a squeal. She turned and saw Katie with a mischievous grin, kicking away from them. Lizzie sent her own splashes toward them, screamed, and swam after Katie when Troy lunged for them. They spent the next several minutes splashing and squealing, until the girls grew tired of the game and scampered out of the pool to try out the slides. Lizzie got to the top of the slide and looked down, her eyes going wide with fear.

"Lizzie, I'll catch you. Why don't you see if you can splash me on your way down?" Troy stepped closer to the end of the slide and held out his arms.

Audrey watched in surprise as Lizzie let go of the edges of the slide and slid right into Troy's arms. Troy caught her, holding her up and twirling her around, letting Lizzie's feet skim the edge of the water. "Want to try that again?"

"Yes! Ten more times." Lizzie was up the ladder quick as a cat and sliding down almost before Troy could get into position.

Audrey laughed as Lizzie caught him off balance, and they both tumbled backwards into the water. The pure joy on Troy's face matched Lizzie's and for a moment, Audrey wondered if she'd ever seen Drew have that much fun with his own daughters. She turned to see Katie standing at the top of the tube slide, her eyes narrowed. Audrey bit her bottom lip, wondering how to remedy the situation. Katie was acting so difficult. One moment she claimed she didn't want anything to do with Troy, and the next she was green with envy watching him play with Lizzie.

Before Audrey could think of what to say though, Troy swam quickly across the pool and slapped the inside of the tube slide. "Hey, Katie, bet you can't get down the slide before I get up there." Troy lifted himself out of the pool and hopped onto the ladder. Katie shrieked and slid down, splashing in the pool and coming out laughing as Troy followed. The scenario repeated several times with Audrey joining in the races down the slides, catching Lizzie, and ducking away from Katie's splashes. Troy had effortlessly circumvented any problems that might've arisen, and Audrey had the feeling that he knew exactly what he was doing. He was trying his best to give equal time to the three of them.

After nearly an hour of splashing, laughing, and swimming, everyone was exhausted. They laid out in the sun and sipped lemonade, chattering about who was the best at slide wars. Audrey reached her hand out for Troy's, squeezing his fingers. "Thank you. This has been the best Fourth of July party I can remember."

Lizzie actually dozed off after Audrey helped her change back into her clothes. The swimming really had tired them out. Troy took them down to the gazebo, where citronella candles and tiki torches surrounded the area in preparation for the fireworks display. Troy helped Audrey settle Lizzie onto a blanket under a magnolia tree. She looked out at the pond and noticed a floating platform next to a small paddleboat. A man in a T-shirt and shorts bent over a pile of multicolored boxes on the platform.

"Is he setting up fireworks on the pond?" Audrey asked.

Troy grinned. "He is. I'm pretty excited for the show."

Katie stepped up next to Audrey and leaned into her. "How will the fireworks light on the water?" She squinted, watching the man setting up the display.

"Remote control. There's another guy working over there." Troy pointed, and sure enough, another man stood on the edge of the banks of the pond, working on something.

"Is anyone else coming?" Katie asked.

"No, this is just for us." He put his arm around Audrey and smiled at Katie. "It's your very own private Fourth of July celebration."

Katie glanced at Troy and then looked back out at the water. "Wow," she said almost reverently.

Joyce brought out more refreshments, and they walked around the gazebo eating cream puffs dotted with blueberries and strawberries.

"It looks like you might have won over Katie before the fireworks have even begun," Audrey said.

"I hope so. I want this to be a memorable experience for her, and you, and Lizzie."

"And what about you? Will this be a memorable experience for you, or have you done this sort of thing before?"

Troy shook his head. "Nope. I've hosted some big bashes, but nothing like this." He took her hand and brought it to his lips, kissing her knuckles.

It was in that moment, as Audrey watched his brown eyes twinkle with excitement as he did something as innocent as kissing her knuckles, that Audrey realized she'd fallen for Troy Jackson. There was still so much she needed to know about him, so much he needed to know about her. But for tonight, she was okay to push her worries out of focus and enjoy the moment he presented her.

When darkness fell, Lizzie woke up with some grumbling until Audrey reminded her that the fireworks would be starting soon. Troy blew out the candles and extinguished the tiki torches so the darkness grew thicker around them.

"I think we need a countdown to start," Troy said as he motioned to the man at the edge of the pond.

The man gave a hand signal, and Troy started counting down from ten. The girls joined in, and Audrey smiled as she chanted the numbers, "Three, two, one!"

A burst of light erupted from the center of the pond, shooting skyward and crackling with white light that turned blue and then red. Everyone cheered.

"Mommy, those are the best fireworks I've ever seen!" Lizzie cried.

"And that was only the first one," Troy replied. He settled back on the blanket, draping his arm around Audrey. She leaned into his chest as the fireworks display continued. Katie clapped and cheered when several purple and pink fireworks exploded in the sky. After nearly thirty minutes of fireworks that exploded, reverberating across the pond so that Audrey felt it in her chest, the show ended with the grand finale. Every color of the rainbow seemed to fill the sky, accompanied by the crackling music of the fireworks dancing together.

"I've never seen a fireworks show like this either," Audrey said. "Thank you so much for tonight."

"Thank you, Audrey." Troy leaned in and kissed her softly. "I'll never forget tonight."

Chapter 14

Audrey felt like she was still lit up inside from the glow of the fireworks; the afterburn in the night sky didn't fade from her heart. When she returned to work on Thursday, it was with happy expectations for her lunch date with Troy. He'd made it a point to carve out time in his busy schedule to take her to lunch. They'd talked and texted a few times over the past couple days, with both of them admitting how much they missed the other. Audrey felt like she was a teenager experiencing her first crush all over again. She didn't try to subdue her smile when she walked past Rachel's desk. The secretary gave her a knowing look and smiled back.

Audrey took a few minutes to go over her notes in preparation for Felicia's coaching session. She would meet with Jake tomorrow, and Mike had asked if he could schedule time to talk to her about the possibility of working with another new singer the following week.

Audrey didn't want to jinx herself by even thinking that she was living the dream she had for so many years, but every morning she woke up, applied her makeup, and stared at herself grinning in the mirror. She wondered how a freckled redhead girl from the Northwest could land in one of the most successful Christian record companies in Nashville.

Two minutes before Felicia's appointment was scheduled to begin, there was a light knock on the door and she stepped in, a big smile on her face. "Audrey, I'm so excited." Felicia bounced on her toes. "I did my homework like you told me. I researched everything on Arise, and looked at Troy Jackson's life." Her lip trembled and her eyes filled with tears. "He *is* a good man. I had no idea everything that he went through, how much he changed his life and in just a few years. I would have never recognized him."

Audrey's skin prickled with fear. "What do you mean? What did you find?"

Felicia hesitated. "Well, wasn't that the stuff you were referring to? His time in jail?"

Audrey clamped her mouth shut. She couldn't mess this up; she needed to learn what Felicia thought she had found, because there was no way Troy Jackson, billionaire and CEO of Arise Music, had spent time in jail. Audrey pasted on a thin smile. "Oh, I wasn't sure what you meant. What part about Troy being in jail impressed you so much?"

"Well, first I wasn't sure if it was him, because back then he went by his nickname. It's a middle name or something. Stone."

"You mean Stone Jackson?" Audrey's heart was hanging on by one thread, and she wasn't sure if she should listen to another word.

"Yeah, that's it. He used to be quite the player. He was the richest playboy around. He had a new girlfriend every other day, and then he got into drugs. He was arrested, all of his assets were frozen, and then while he was in jail, he came to know Christ. That's what impressed me. He fell so far, he was living the life of a sinner and acting like he was enjoying it. And then he changed everything. He hasn't even dated anyone since."

Audrey sat down in the chair, her head pounding with the words Felicia spoke that couldn't be true.

"Are you okay? You look a little pale."

"I'm suddenly not feeling very good. Maybe we could reschedule?"

"Sure. Mike wanted me to see if I could squeeze a little more time out of my day, so this will actually work well. Just text me and we'll get it set up." She squeezed Audrey's arm. "Thank you again for helping me make the right decision. I hope you feel better."

Audrey nodded, not trusting herself to speak. She waited until Felicia left her office before she opened up the search bar and typed in Stone Jackson. Immediately the screen was filled with links to numerous articles and images of him. She'd heard of Stone Jackson, of the party boy who'd finally gotten caught, and the many people who hated him. With trembling fingers, Audrey clicked on an image search for Stone Jackson.

Her throat felt like she was swallowing chalk as she leaned closer to the screen to see the pictures of Stone Jackson, the man Audrey only knew as Troy. Troy Stone Jackson, his middle name after his mother's maiden name. He was raised in a good family, a good Christian family, but as a teenager, he decided to live life on his own terms.

Audrey scanned the rest of his bio; some of the things were familiar, like how Troy said he'd made his fortune early with smart investments. He'd bought out struggling companies and revitalized them. Other parts seemed like a made-up story, but the truth of the photos couldn't be denied. Stone Jackson had been a player, a rich, spoiled young man who could afford to have a new girlfriend every week. He'd traveled the world picking up women in exotic locales, and his wild life came to a crashing halt when he was arrested for drug possession five years ago.

Audrey didn't want to read it. She didn't want to see the photos of him. He was so different. His hair was long, dyed black, and he had piercings in his nose and several in both ears. In most of the pictures he had his arm around a woman and a smirk on his face. If Felicia hadn't been the one to tell her, Audrey might not have recognized that Stone Jackson was also Troy Jackson. But as she scrolled through the photos, the pit in her stomach turned to a gaping cavern. After less than ten minutes, Audrey closed out the screens with disgust. The taste of betrayal was acrid in her mouth as she thought of Troy kissing her, of the night he wouldn't hold her because he was waiting for marriage. The heat of embarrassment crept across her skin and it flicked the switch to anger.

Audrey smacked her forehead with her palm. "How could I be so stupid?"

Tears stung her eyes and she closed them, covering her mouth with her hand, trying to swallow the sob working its way up her throat. Troy was exactly like Drew, using women at everyone else's expense. A tiny voice crept into Audrey's head reminding her of what else she had seen on the internet. Yes, Troy had been a playboy and he'd been arrested for drug possession, but then he'd reformed his life. He'd changed everything. He'd even made public statements, apologizing to all the people—especially the women—he'd hurt with his reckless behavior. He'd set up a new women's shelter in Nashville, fully funded by Arise Music, and he'd hired ambassadors from several churches to create a campaign for honoring women.

One of the headlines had read: ***Stone Jackson Turns His Life over to God.***

Audrey wanted to believe that, but why hadn't Troy told her about his past? Especially when he found out how skittish she was around men because of what Drew had done to her. He should've told her. Audrey stood and gripped the back of the chair, standing with her knees locked until she felt lightheaded, her world crumbling around her. It was all true. Everything Felicia had said was true.

Audrey gathered up her things, walked out into the lobby, and paused at Rachel's desk. "Rachel, I need you to cancel all of my appointments for the rest of the week."

Rachel looked up, the smile on her face faltering when she saw Audrey's expression. "Oh dear, you don't look good at all. Are you sick?"

Audrey nodded. "Yes," was all she could manage before she bolted for the door. Her chin trembled, and tears leaked from her eyes as she got into her car. Audrey swiped at them, angry that she'd allowed another man to hurt her. Never again.

She drove back to her quiet house. She couldn't pick up the girls in this state; she needed time to sort out the ugly truth that was working hard to beat her down. She walked into the kitchen from the garage, and Duke greeted her as soon as she walked in the door. Audrey broke down then, sliding to the floor, putting her arm around Duke as she cried.

Her dog was quiet. He put his head against hers and whined, and for some reason, that made Audrey cry harder. She wasn't sure how long she sat there with Duke; time passed slowly in her agony. Then she heard a knock at her door.

Audrey checked her watch. It was just after twelve, and she definitely wasn't expecting anyone since she was supposed to be at work. When Audrey checked the peephole, she felt the blood drain from her face. Troy Jackson stood on her front steps, his face lined with anxiety. Audrey had learned one thing from dealing with Drew: it was better to face her demons and exorcise them quickly. Duke padded up next to her, his tongue lolling to the side.

"Duke, be good," she said. She opened the door and stepped back. "Come in, Troy. I'll make this quick."

"Audrey, are you okay?" Troy stepped in and she closed the door behind him. "Rachel said you left in a hurry and you looked terribly sick, but she didn't know what was wrong. I've been trying to call. I was worried."

"How sad for you," Audrey said flatly.

Troy pulled back. "What happened? You're trembling. You look so angry."

"How could you, Troy?" Audrey covered her face with her hands and took a shuddering breath. Unbidden, she remembered the night she'd discovered that Drew had cheated on her not once, but with multiple women. She'd felt like garbage. And even then, Drew had promised to change—promised not to hurt her again. She hated all the lies, and even as she tried to bring herself back to the present and separate the hurt from her past, Audrey felt like her heart had been pierced by a dozen arrows.

She let her hands fall to her side, clenching them into fists. "How could you use me like this? I trusted you." Audrey's lip started to shake, and she couldn't keep the tears from falling again. Duke whined and pushed his head against her hand.

Troy glanced at the dog and then back at Audrey. "I think I know what this is about." Troy's voice dropped to a whisper. "Felicia told me how you talked to her about making the right decision. She said you urged her to look into what kind of company we were."

"Yes, Troy, that's right. Or should I call you Stone?" Audrey spat. "The craziest thing about this is Felicia is totally great with sticking with your company, but now I'm not."

Troy stepped forward, his hands out. "Audrey, I'm not Stone anymore. That's all in the past."

She clenched her fists tighter. "Why didn't you tell me? I deserved to know."

"I was scared. I've been scared ever since our first date that you wouldn't give me a chance." Troy pushed his hand through his hair. "I'm not Stone anymore. I didn't tell you because it doesn't have anything to do with us."

"Yes it does. It's called trust. And I have a problem with it. How can I trust a man who did what you did? You were in jail, Troy! You've done everything!"

"I've repented of that," Troy said quietly, his eyes dropping to the floor.

"I still deserved to know."

His head snapped up, his eyes bright with moisture. "So are you going to tell me every sin you've ever committed? Or are you perfect?"

Audrey clenched her jaw, anger burning through her chest. "You lied to me by not telling me."

Troy pursed his lips and blew out a breath. "You're right. I was a monster. I did everything wrong. But I've changed."

"Well, good for you. Maybe you'll find a woman who hasn't been burned by a man who claims he can change. Maybe you can find someone to date who doesn't mind that you used women like playthings. You're just like my ex-husband! I don't want anything to do with you." Audrey threw her hands in the air, backing away from him.

"Hold on. Now you're just being cruel. You know I'm not like your ex. He doesn't want anything to do with your daughters. How could anyone be so coldhearted as to ignore their existence? Audrey, I love you. I love Katie and Lizzie. I'm sorry I didn't tell you. I promise you that it was on my mind. I was trying to find the right time to talk to you. Please, can't you respect that I needed to know you well enough before I opened that door?"

"I don't want to hear your excuses, Troy." Audrey's voice was flat.

"Don't punish me because you're scared. We can work through this." He reached out and put his hands on Audrey's shoulders. She jerked away.

"Don't touch me!" She walked back to the front door and opened it. "I'm glad you came by. It was the right thing to do. Now you need to leave."

"Audrey, please don't do this. We can work this out. I'll do anything. Please don't do anything drastic." Troy stood there, his eyes full of hurt and confusion.

Audrey shook her head. "You need to leave."

"Okay, I'll leave now. But please just think about it." Troy backed out slowly, as if hoping she would change her mind and invite him to stay, but Audrey shut the door and leaned against it. Duke whined softly and licked her ankles. She slid down on the floor and cried into his coarse hair.

Chapter 15

It was Mike's words that Troy heard first in his mind as he drove away from Audrey's house. He remembered how his friend had urged him to tell Audrey all the sordid details of his past, and Troy hadn't listened because he thought he had more time. Troy shook his head. The way Audrey had reacted, it probably wouldn't have mattered if he had told her about Stone Jackson, the person he wasn't anymore. Her eyes had been so cold, hard, and unforgiving. He didn't want to think about it, but he couldn't ignore the pain radiating from his heart, searing every nerve throughout his body. He loved Audrey, loved her girls, and he wanted to be part of their life. He sped home as quickly as he could, blinking away the tears that kept welling up in his eyes. When he got home, he didn't go inside; instead, he walked out to the gazebo and sat on the white bench. He bit his lip and closed his eyes, trying to hold himself together, but the emotions crashed against him, begging to be released.

Troy leaned forward, put his head in his hands, and began praying. "Please, God, please. If there is any way you can help her, please help her to forgive me." He whispered the words again and again, wishing there was a way to stop the pain that flared with every beat of his heart.

Audrey rejected all of Troy's calls. She deleted his voicemail messages without listening to them because working at Arise Music didn't seem like a possibility anymore. She even thought about blocking his number so that he couldn't text her, but she didn't. She gave in and read a few of his texts, begging for a chance to explain to her just how much he'd changed. She saved one of his texts and read it over a few times

Audrey, I love you. I love you more than I even realized and I'm so scared now that I know that because I can't lose you. You and Katie and Lizzie have been the best part of every day lately. Please talk to me. I'll do anything. I just need a chance to show you how much I love you.

The message tempted her to talk to him, but the wounded side of her heart wouldn't allow it. Somehow, she made it through the weekend, and when LuAnne checked on her, Audrey told her that she and Troy had broken up, but she couldn't talk about it. LuAnne made her promise to come over first thing Monday morning to talk.

After breakfast on Monday, Audrey took her girls over to LuAnne's house. While the kids played, she sat with her best friend at the kitchen table and told her everything that she'd discovered about Troy—the man who was also Stone Jackson.

LuAnne shook her head. "Stone Jackson. I can't hardly believe it, but now that you say it, I knew that Troy looked familiar. I just couldn't figure out why."

"And when he came to my house, I couldn't … I asked him to leave."

"That's been at least five years." LuAnne touched Audrey's arm, "I think he was telling the truth."

Audrey narrowed her eyes. "But he didn't tell me the truth. He didn't tell me anything until I found out about his past." She pushed her bangs off of her forehead and leaned forward into her hand. "I don't understand why it didn't bother Felicia. She actually seemed happy finding out that he was this horrible person."

"Perhaps it's because it made him human. Troy isn't a god," LuAnne said. "To most people, he's incredibly powerful, successful, and wealthy. To see that he made mistakes just like all of us probably helped her feel better about working with him."

"It doesn't make me feel better. I don't want to ever see him again," Audrey said.

"Do you really mean that? I mean, have you given yourself time to process your emotions, separate your fears from reality?" LuAnne looked her in the eye, and Audrey couldn't be angry at her friend's direct approach, because it was obvious how much LuAnne cared for her.

"I don't know. I know I can't do this, I can't be hurt again." Audrey leaned back in the chair and folded her arms. "I have to take care of my family first."

LuAnne leaned forward. "*You* are part of that family, Audrey. Your happiness is integral to the success of your family. These past few weeks when you've been dating Troy, it's the happiest I've ever seen you."

"So you're saying I should just ignore everything? Just stay with Troy because I was happy, oblivious to everything?"

"No, I'm saying that you should figure this out. You should work on this, find out if you can trust him. Find out if Troy's worth it."

Audrey lifted her head and frowned. "If I had come to you and told you that I was thinking about dating the man who used to be Stone Jackson, what would you have told me?"

LuAnne tucked a strand of hair behind her ear, her fingers resting against the dark skin of her cheek. "I would ask you what kind of man he is now. I hope that I would tell you to be careful, but to be fair. Has Troy given you any indication that he wants to return to his old lifestyle?"

Audrey bit her lip, not wanting to answer LuAnne's question because she was slowly building evidence in favor of Troy. She blew out a breath. "No, he would barely even hold me. He told me about how he'd made commitments, and he wanted to keep them. He's been perfect. That's the problem: I should've seen it. Troy was too perfect."

LuAnne chuckled. "Well, that just means you don't know him well enough, because nobody's perfect."

Audrey rubbed a hand over her swollen eyes and looked up at the ceiling. "I don't know what to do."

"Maybe you should try praying," LuAnne said softly.

Audrey sat up, looking directly at LuAnne. Her friend was very religious, one of the strongest Christians Audrey knew, but early on in their friendship they'd agreed that they wouldn't discuss religion. It was hard for LuAnne, but she'd honored

Audrey's request. "I don't think now is the time for me to get chummy with God."

LuAnne laughed. "Well, it's the only piece of advice I can give you that will actually work. This situation is just too hard to do on your own."

Audrey shook her head. "No, I think it's better if I leave God out of it." She swallowed back harsh words that she wanted to say—she respected her friend too much to say them. But the words still trailed through her mind. How she felt that God had abandoned her because he let Drew hurt her so deeply.

As if LuAnne could read her thoughts, she asked, "Audrey, do you think you could ever forgive Drew for what he did to you?"

Audrey straightened. "What? What does that have to do with this, with Troy?"

"I think it may have a lot more to do with it than you realize."

"Drew deserves to burn. I don't have to give him anything," Audrey spat. Hurt and anger welled up inside her, mixing with the fresh wounds Troy had inflicted.

LuAnne reached out and squeezed her hand. "You won't give him anything, but you'll give yourself freedom from him. Forgiving him doesn't mean you allow him to hurt you again; it just means you give away everything that he did to you. You give it to God so that He can take care of it for you."

"Lu, I thought we had an agreement about this."

LuAnne nodded. "We do, and I respect you enough to be honest with you right now. I want you to go home, leave your girls here for a few hours. Take some time for yourself and look into your heart."

"No, I need my girls to keep me busy, to keep my mind off everything," Audrey protested.

"Just a few hours."

"It won't do any good. I already told you, I can't let Troy hurt me again."

"But has he really hurt you?" LuAnne pushed her finger against the table. "He's still the same man today despite what he did in his past. From where I sit, nothing has changed but your feelings for him."

"Everything has changed. I found out that Troy is just like Drew." Audrey narrowed her eyes. "He's a sinner who claims to know God while treating other people like playthings."

She watched LuAnne's lips twitch at her harsh words, but her friend didn't say anything for a moment. The words Audrey had just spoken settled against her heart like a rock, all sharp edges and jagged lines, and she wanted it that way, because she didn't want to let anyone else near her heart again.

LuAnne breathed in and out slowly and then tapped her index finger on the table. "My Savior, Jesus Christ, consorted with sinners. He forgave them, and he saw them for who they were, people who had made mistakes. People who wanted to do better." LuAnne clasped her hands together as if in a prayer and looked down at her fingers.

Her words felt like soft rain on Audrey shoulders, and she found herself relaxing, the tenseness of the moment draining away. Audrey couldn't argue with what LuAnne said, because it was true. She didn't push the words away; she left them sitting on her shoulders so that she could think about them later.

"Okay, I'll take some time. I'll think about things." She stood slowly, and her friend stood next to her, hesitant.

Audrey reached out and hugged LuAnne. "I may not get along very well with God, but I'm smart enough to realize that He sent me you. Thank you for being my friend, Lu."

LuAnne hugged her back, sighing. "Thank you for being mine. You'd better hurry on out of here before I start giving you my Sunday School lesson."

Both women laughed, but Audrey did as she was told and walked quickly down the street toward her home. Duke greeted her at the door and followed her through the kitchen and then upstairs to her room. Audrey lay across her bed, thinking about the conversation she'd just had and how LuAnne had reminded her of things she hadn't thought about for a long time. She didn't realize that she'd started crying again until Duke nudged her hand, licking her palm. The tears had been her constant companion since Thursday. She'd cried more in the last few days than she had in the last two years.

That was the strange part: when she thought back on the time when she discovered Drew's infidelity, she had cried some, but mostly she had raged. She had nursed her anger and let it fuel her divorce and the cross-country move. She thought she had let go of the anger as her life improved, but every time she had contact with Drew, her stomach would start boiling with hatred for him and all that he had done to her and her girls. More than once she'd wished she could just be rid of it all, not ever have to think of him again. LuAnne's words circled around that thought, the question she'd asked, if Audrey had forgiven Drew so that she *could* let him go.

Audrey slid to her knees beside her bed, clasping her hands together she began to pray for the first time in two years. Duke stood at her side, resting his muzzle next to her hands as if he were praying right along with her. Audrey recalled LuAnne's words, letting them roll across the jagged edges of her rock-hard heart. And she prayed until her knees and back ached, until the tears were all dried up. She asked for help to forgive Drew, and then to forgive Troy and see him as God wanted her to see him.

When she was almost ready to give up, she cried out one last time and felt a warmth encircle her, her chest filling with what she could only describe as light. There was a tremor around her heart, and Audrey imagined it cracking open, bursting from the shell it had been hiding in. She hugged Duke and fresh tears sprang to her eyes, but these tears weren't hot with anger or disappointment. The tears she cried now were cleansing, freeing. Audrey settled on the bed, and Duke hopped up next to her. He licked her hand, and she patted his head.

"Thanks for praying with me, Duke." It was a funny thing to say, but that's exactly what Audrey felt her dog had been doing. He'd stood beside her for over an hour, as if knowing that she needed his support. Audrey searched her heart, and she knew that things would be different from now on. She was ready to change, but she wasn't quite sure how to approach Troy after so many days of ignoring him. She closed her eyes, thinking about what she might say to him when she saw him again. For some reason a Frisbee came to mind, and Audrey smiled.

Chapter 16

Troy was such a wreck by Monday morning that Mike told him he better not come back to work until he'd figured out his love life. And while he was at it, he'd better convince the new vocal coach not to quit her job. Troy had tried everything he could think of to talk to Audrey. He'd even sent her emails, but she wouldn't respond to any of his attempts. She hadn't come into work, and she canceled all of her appointments. Troy was devastated, but he was determined that his past mistakes wouldn't hurt anyone. He knew how much the job meant to Audrey, and if she couldn't work for him anymore, then at least he could help her find another job. So Troy spent a few hours on the phone Monday afternoon, talking with some of his colleagues, putting out feelers in Audrey's behalf. By the end of the day he had two solid leads, and he'd made a decision. Tomorrow, he would drive out to Franklin and try one last time to talk to Audrey. If there was no hope for them, he would let her go and give her the information he'd collected so that she could still work in the recording industry as a vocal coach.

On Tuesday morning, instead of going to work, Troy drove to Audrey's house. No one answered the door. For a second, his heart seized, and he wondered if she'd already left for the day, or worse, left town. But then he shook his head. Lizzie's bike was parked against the side of the house. They must have just run an errand. It was a little after eight o'clock in the morning, so Troy had figured Audrey would be home. He sighed, his shoulders slumping. Maybe it was a sign that he should let her go.

He ripped out a piece of paper from a yellow legal pad in his car, intent on getting the message to Audrey one way or another. He would end everything today and disappear from her life. The last thing he wanted to do was hurt her. He sat on the front step, holding a pen in his hand, trying to think of the right words to put to paper. He wrote the note, carefully creased the paper, and slid the paper through her front door. Troy turned to go, resignation weighing down his steps.

Then he heard Duke barking in the backyard. The dog barked, yipped, and barked again. Troy walked around back and fiddled with the gate until he was able to get in the backyard. There was no sign of Audrey or her girls, but Duke trotted over to him.

"What are you doing here, boy?" Troy asked, and he figured that Duke would've asked him the same thing if the dog could speak. Troy couldn't see any reason for Duke to be barking. There were no other animals in the backyard and no other people around. Duke licked his palm, and his tail wagged affectionately. Troy walked across the backyard and sat on the grass next to the new magnolia tree that Audrey had told him about. He leaned his head forward and rested on his knees. "I'll never be able to have a normal life," he whispered.

Because of him, Audrey's life was in pieces. He should've left her alone, but he couldn't resist. Even though he'd changed, he couldn't really expect people to take him seriously. His heart was in need of the kind of love only Audrey could offer him. But she had refused, and he couldn't help her trust that he wasn't exactly like her ex-husband. "I should've told her when I had a chance," Troy said as he lifted his head.

Duke whined and leaned against Troy. "You're a good boy," Troy said. It was as if Duke could sense how Troy was feeling. A couple minutes passed, and then Troy got up, brushed off his pants, and patted Duke on the head. "Take care of her, okay?"

Duke whined again, and Troy scratched behind the dog's ears for a moment before hurrying back out the gate and getting in his car. As he drove away from Audrey's house, he could hardly breathe through the pain, but he forced himself to keep going. He prayed mightily that there could still be a chance for him and Audrey. Troy turned on his radio and listened to Jake Mendez sing a song about the Redeemer. He let the words and the music caress his broken heart as he drove back to his mansion, alone.

Chapter 17

When Audrey arrived home, she found Duke in the kitchen, his tail wagging with as close to a smile as a dog can get. As his tail moved back and forth, it swished bits of paper across the floor.

"Duke, what have you been doing?" Audrey asked. She bent down and picked up a scrap of paper. The handwriting was unfamiliar. It wasn't from a bill or any of her personal papers. "Where did this come from?"

Duke barked and ran a quick circle around the kitchen before sitting down again in front of Audrey. His tail resumed wagging, scattering more papers across the floor. Audrey examined the piece in her hand. It was wet from Duke's mouth.

"Did you eat my mail?" She snatched another piece of paper as it fluttered past her. This one wasn't wet and soggy and she could actually make out the words on the paper. Audrey smoothed the paper out and read aloud, "I'll never."

She got on her hands and knees and crawled around Duke, picking up several scraps of paper that had been completely destroyed. Her hands stilled when she saw Troy's signature on a piece that had evidently come from the bottom of the note. Audrey sat down on the floor, holding the chewed-up bits of paper in her hands. What did this mean? She had ignored every one of Troy's efforts to reach her. He must have stopped by today and hand-delivered this note. She smoothed out another piece of paper that was no more than two inches wide. Troy's handwriting was bold, written with a black pen. She read the words *let you go*. Audrey's heart picked up speed as she carefully held out the first piece and put it next to the second piece.

"I'll never let you go." Audrey swallowed, trying to sort through the tornado of emotions swirling through her mind. She had rejected Troy in every way that she could. She'd been cruel to him when she should've been kind. Instead of letting her go, he had come by today to tell her that he would never give up. How did he know that was what Audrey needed most of all? She needed someone who would never give up, who would believe in her when she didn't believe in herself.

Audrey scrambled around her kitchen, gathering up the last few scraps of paper. She smoothed out what she could on the table, but despite her best efforts she couldn't read any more of the message. Duke had likely ingested most of the note. If she really wanted to find out what the note said, she would have to contact Troy. A shimmer of anxiety ran along her nerves as Audrey studied out the choice she needed to make.

Either she could forgive Troy as LuAnne had suggested, or she could let him go forever. It wasn't a simple choice. The ramifications were far-reaching, including her dream job.

She began scrubbing her kitchen, trying to sort through all that had happened in less than a week. The one thing that stood out above the rest was Troy's declaration of love for her. Everything he had done indicated that his love was patient and strong. Her mother had warned her once, when she was young, not to let fear rule her life. Even though Audrey didn't want to admit it, that's exactly what had happened. Fear had pushed her onto the path she was on now, because she was so afraid of being hurt again, because Drew had crushed her belief in men and made her afraid to love again. Audrey knew the choice that fear would have her make, to shut Troy out of her life, giving him no access to injure her heart. When she separated herself from fear and looked at the situation through a new lens, Audrey knew what she should do. The question was, did she really have the courage to do it?

Duke nudged her leg and whined softly. Audrey turned and crouched in front of him. "What is it, boy?"

He whined and pushed his muzzle against her hand, licking her wrist. Duke stopped and stared at Audrey, his dark eyes imploring her to understand what he needed. But then as she looked into his eyes, she remembered the first time she'd seen him at the animal shelter. He was a stray dog, an abandoned puppy brought to the shelter and he'd looked at her with those soulful eyes begging for a second chance at life. And Audrey and her daughters had given Duke that chance. They loved him and he loved them back. Duke had a past, certainly some connection to another dog or person, but he loved her and her family intensely. Audrey didn't know all of the details of Duke's past, but she loved him just the same. She leaned forward, hugging Duke, understanding what he'd wanted her to know.

Audrey's kitchen was spotless, and the girls were watching another Disney movie by the time she picked up her phone and dialed Troy's number.

"Audrey? Is it really you?" he asked.

Audrey sucked in a breath, not realizing she'd been holding hers until she heard Troy's voice. "Yes, it's me. I'm calling because I wanted to tell you I'm sorry I haven't been fair to you. I've done a lot of thinking. I believe you. I believe that you're a different man."

"Did you read my note, then?"

Audrey glanced at the fragments of paper on her dining room table. "Well, the thing is, Duke ate your note. But I read the most important parts."

"And what part was that?"

"The part where you said you'd never let me go. That's what I needed to hear. I needed to hear that you wouldn't give up on me."

"Audrey, can I come over there? Can I see you tonight?"

A familiar thrill shot through Audrey's stomach at the earnestness in his voice. "That depends, I guess, on whether you're bringing dinner or not?" She infused a teasing lilt to her voice.

Troy chuckled. "I'll be there as soon as I can with dinner *and* dessert."

"Good. We have a lot to talk about."

"Thank you, Audrey. Thank you for giving me a second chance."

"See you soon." Audrey squeezed the phone to her chest after she ended the call. She glanced around the room. At least her house was clean, and she had enough time to shower and make herself presentable before Troy arrived.

Troy drove as fast as he dared to get to Audrey's house. He left work over an hour early to beat rush-hour traffic. He still wasn't sure what had happened. He'd written the note, but nowhere in it did he say, *I'll never let you go*. He racked his brain, trying to think of what lines Audrey must've read. He remembered writing something about "I'll never forgive myself," and later on in his letter telling her that he would let her go if that's what she wanted him to do. He shook his head. It didn't really matter what had happened, because he was on his way to Audrey's. He looked forward to the chance to talk with her openly.

He pulled into her driveway just before six o'clock and jogged up the front steps, the brown paper bags full of hamburgers and fries tickling his nostrils as he stood at the front door. When Audrey opened the front door, Troy didn't hesitate. He stepped inside, dropped the sacks, and pulled her into her his arms. "I've missed you so much it hurts."

Audrey nodded against his chest, hugging him tight. "Me, too."

Troy saw Duke, out of the corner of his eye, start to nose in one of the sacks. "Not now, Duke. I brought something special for you." He lifted up two of the brown sacks and handed them to Audrey. "These are for us." Then he picked up the smaller brown paper bag. "This is for Duke."

"Well, let's go on into the kitchen. You can feed Duke in the mud room." Audrey smiled up at Troy and walked slowly into the kitchen as if waiting for him to catch up with her.

Troy felt the connection to her like a tether. He didn't want to be apart from her either. He gave Duke a bone and patted his head. "Thanks for saving me, buddy." Duke lifted his head and looked Troy in the eyes for a second before returning to his bone.

When Troy returned to the kitchen, Audrey and the girls were seated at the table. "Will you offer the prayer?" Audrey said.

Troy's mouth dropped open, but when he saw that she was serious, he nodded. He offered a simple prayer, and the girls loaded up their paper plates with food. He kept glancing at Audrey, wondering what had happened.

"I can hear the questions in your mind," Audrey murmured. "I discovered something over the last few days, and I asked God if He and I could be friends again."

Troy smiled. "I'm so glad to hear that."

"I feel so much better. Your note couldn't have come at a better time." She reached over and squeezed his hand.

"I want you to know that I was in the depths of despair," Troy said. "I prayed for help, for one more chance to talk to you, and God sent me a dog. Not just any dog—but a stray dog who found a family to protect."

Audrey arched an eyebrow. "He sent you a dog?"

"Yep, he sent me Duke." Troy chuckled. Duke heard his name and came out of the washroom, tail wagging. Troy patted his head and fed him a French fry. "Duke saved me from making a big mistake. When I came by this morning, I was ready to let you go, leave everything behind. Duke changed my letter to what I really wanted to say."

Audrey looked down at her plate and swallowed. "Then we've both been saved by a stray dog, because Duke saved me too." Audrey put her arm around the dog's neck and hugged him. "He listened to me when there was no one else to talk to. I have a feeling he understands more than we could ever imagine."

"I'll agree with that," Troy said. "Audrey, I'm willing to share anything with you that you want to know. You can ask me anything, and I'll answer it honestly."

Audrey shook her head. "I don't need to know that. All I need to know is who you are now, and who you hope to be tomorrow."

Troy leaned over and kissed Audrey. "The luckiest man in the world, today and tomorrow."

Chapter 18

~ One Month Later

Troy paced back and forth under a magnolia tree in the park, waiting for Audrey to arrive. His nerves were popping like firecrackers, and he kept having to bite back the smile that stretched from ear to ear.

A few minutes later, he saw her walking through the park with her daughters and Duke. Troy waved and headed in their direction. "How are my favorite ladies and one gentleman?"

Katie and Lizzie laughed, giving him a quick hug. Audrey kissed his cheek. "Just fine today. How about you?"

"I think I'm about to get a whole lot better." He took Audrey's oversized bag from her, ignoring her curious glance, and helped them to the spot he'd set up for a picnic.

"Duke, will you help me with something?" Troy asked, and Duke perked up his ears. Troy turned to Audrey, his smile widening. "I wonder if he's been working on his game of fetch?" Now Duke stood and yipped.

Audrey laughed. "He gets better every day."

Troy nodded and patted Duke's head. "Well, that's good, because I was hoping by now he's learned how to fetch a fiancée."

Audrey gasped, her eyes widening. "What are you saying?"

Troy knelt down, his body filled with music that played in time to Audrey's every breath. "Audrey, marry me? Please." Troy held out a white box and flipped open the lid. The sunlight hit the diamond and scattered sparkles in all directions.

Audrey put a hand over her mouth, her eyes filling with tears. Duke yipped again and put his paw on Troy's hand. Troy smiled. "We're both waiting for your answer."

Audrey launched herself into Troy's arms. "Yes! Yes, I'll marry you."

"Mommy's getting married!" Lizzie cheered. "Troy is gonna be our new daddy!"

Troy turned to catch Katie's reaction, and her smile looked like it could compete with the diamond's sparkles. "Aren't you going to kiss her?"

Troy laughed and kissed Audrey, holding her close, never wanting to let her go. Audrey giggled, and Troy felt Duke's wet tongue across his cheek. "Not quite how I pictured the moment, but it'll do."

Audrey stepped away, picked up a Frisbee, and threw it as hard as she could. "Duke, fetch!" Duke took off running after the Frisbee, the girls squealing and running after him. Audrey turned to Troy with a twinkle in her eye. "Now, where were we?"

Troy grinned and pulled the most beautiful woman he knew in for another kiss.

160

The End

If you enjoyed this Billionaire Romance from Rachelle J. Christensen, you may also enjoy her other sweet romance series, Burke Billionaire Romance. Enjoy this sneak peek of book #1 *Hawaiian Masquerade*.

Chapter 1

Lexi stared at the tube of cadmium red oil paint hanging from the shelf, remembering how expensive that color had seemed in college. She grabbed it and ten additional tubes in a rainbow of colors—the first step on a new path in life. The squeaking wheel of the shopping cart gave voice to the trepidation crawling up her spine, telling her she was nuts for leaving behind a life that most people claimed they wanted. But Lexi knew something that most people didn't: millions and millions of dollars did not create a wellspring of happiness. Cold hard cash was, in fact, cold and hard.

Kauai was not cold. The brilliant sunshine and perfumed air was freely available to everyone on the island. Roadways were drenched in color from vibrant greens to bright pinks and accented with the red dirt Kauai was known for. Lexi studied the brushes available and chose a long-handled round brush that would help her recreate the beautiful landscapes of the island. Now if she could find a few canvases, she would be ready to paint on the beach outside her home. She turned down another aisle and saw a display of white rectangles and squares. They were wrapped in plastic, but Lexi ran her finger along the edges; the rough feel of a blank canvas and the possibility it represented brought back pleasant memories.

A toddler's shrill cry snapped her out of her musings. She steered her cart around a stack of twelve-by-eighteen-inch canvases and found the source. The little girl couldn't have been more than two years old, tiny with fine black hair pulled back in pigtails. Her red hibiscus-print dress set off dark caramel skin, and even as her wail intensified, Lexi found herself admiring the pretty Polynesian girl.

That's when she noticed that the toddler was alone. Lexi glanced around, but this area of the store was empty. She stepped forward carefully and crouched in front of the girl. "Sweetie, are you lost?"

As soon as the words left her mouth, the little girl held out her arms and reached for Lexi. She sniffled, melting Lexi's heart as she carefully picked up the child. She looked down the aisle, hoping to see the little girl's mother, but at the same time nervous that the mother would think her daughter was being kidnapped. Lexi patted the girl's back, and she snuggled closer. Swallowing against the sudden lump in her throat, Lexi focused on the task at hand.

Turning slowly to scan the store again, she saw a man with dark hair, a chiseled jawline, and a worried crease in his forehead. He was tall with golden-brown skin and wore a green tank top that showed off his finely sculpted biceps. Something shifted in Lexi's heart. It thumped hard twice, and blood rose to her cheeks. The man stared back at her, his face open, revealing an arc of emotions as he took in the sight of the little girl and Lexi—wonder, admiration, curiosity, and something else she couldn't define.

She stepped forward, eyebrows raised in question. "Is she yours?"

His dark hair was spiked on top and close-shaven on the sides. He sported a bit of scruff that Lexi could only describe as sexy. One side of his mouth lifted, and he shook his head. "No, is she lost?"

"Yes, she was crying right over here, and I've stayed put for a minute hoping her mom would show up looking for her."

He turned around in a slow circle, repeating the search Lexi had undertaken moments before, having a better view over the shelves because he was taller. Oh, so tall and sculpted. "I can help you find her parents. This store isn't that big. Maybe they haven't missed her yet."

Lexi's brow furrowed in protest as she struggled to rein in her emotions. It had been at least three minutes since she'd heard the toddler's cries, and five minutes was like an eternity in a child's world—surely it would feel just as long for a frantic parent searching for her child. She gently patted the girl's back. "It's okay, sweetie, I know what it feels like to be lost," she murmured. Then she realized that the man was standing close enough to hear her. She straightened, cleared her throat, and spoke louder. "We'll help you."

The man pointed to the other side of the store. "I'll go this way, you go that way?"

"That's a good idea." Lexi smiled, and her stomach flipped when the man returned her smile. The little girl moved her head, quiet and warm in Lexi's arms.

The man walked quickly across the store, and Lexi went in the other direction. There was only one other shopper, an old man with a handful of charcoal and sketch pads. Lexi smiled at him, and he winked at her and the little girl. "Beautiful kaikamahine."

Lexi nodded, appreciating the melodic Hawaiian language. The man saw them as mother and daughter, which was a stretch considering Lexi's fair skin, blond hair, and green eyes. She held the child close. They were two lost souls trying to find something to keep them safe. Lexi was certain she'd find the little girl's mother, but what could Lexi find that would fill the need in her heart?

"Here she is," someone said from behind Lexi. She turned around and saw that the dark-haired man was leading a Polynesian woman with long dark hair toward her. "Safe and sound."

"Keilani! Oh, baby," the woman said. "I'm so glad you're okay."

The little girl immediately sat up and reached her arms out. She cried for a few seconds, clinging to her mother, clutching her light cotton shirt.

"Mahalo. Oh, thank you so much for finding my baby," the woman gushed.

"She's a sweetheart," Lexi said. "She wanted me to hold her, and that seemed to help while we looked for you."

"One minute she was there, and then she was gone. You know how kids are." The woman patted her daughter's back. "Keilani, say thank you to the beautiful lady who found you," the woman said, looking down at her daughter with a smile.

The toddler looked at Lexi and held her hand out, moving it back and forth. Then she giggled and blew Lexi a kiss.

Lexi pretended to catch the kiss in the air and patted her cheek. "Thank you, Keilani. Have fun shopping."

She waved at the little girl, then let her hand drop to her side. That's when she noticed the man who had helped her standing quietly next to the end cap of paintbrushes on aisle seven. "You really get the credit for finding her," Lexi said. "Thanks for hunting down the lost mother."

He grinned. "Glad to help out a tourist when I can."

"But I'm not a tourist," Lexi replied. "I just moved here."

One eyebrow lifted, and Lexi noticed a shift in his brown eyes, as if he were seeing her for the first time. He held out his hand. "That's great news. Aloha, and welcome to Kauai. I'm Derek Mitchell."

They shook hands, and a sensation like warm, salty spray went up her arm. When they broke contact, she immediately craved his touch again. What was happening to her? The first hot guy to shake her hand had her thinking of moonlight walks on the beach and kisses in the sand. She decided that she was smitten with the *idea* of this Hawaiian guy. She needed a can of chocolate-covered macadamia nuts and a long bath, not a man. Still, she smiled broadly and returned the introduction. "I'm Lexi Burke, no longer from Chicago."

Derek wrinkled his nose. "Man, that place is cold. Good choice coming here in March. The weather will only get better from now until October."

"I'm counting on it," Lexi replied.

"Are you an artist?" Derek asked, motioning to the growing stack of supplies in Lexi's cart, which she'd left in the middle of the aisle.

"I wish." Lexi laughed as she grabbed the handle. "Maybe in a different lifetime—or maybe now. I love art, and I need to refocus some of my energy. Drawing and painting used to be a passion of mine, before the nine-to-five killed it."

Derek nodded. "I get that. The good thing about this place is it unwinds all that tension, and creativity leaks out from everywhere." He tipped his head to the side. "Since you're new, I'll let you in on a secret. Drive over to Hanapepe tomorrow—Friday night is the local art night—and you'll see what I mean."

"Hmm, I may just do that." Lexi gave Derek her canned response to every invite from the male species. And then she realized that he was being friendly. Maybe she could go . . . but then she might run into him, and he was too good-looking with that bronzed skin and his relaxed stance that seemed to say, *I don't have any idea what my looks do to your pulse rate.* Yep. Derek was on her list of things not to encounter in Kauai. Her fingertips drummed along the plastic-wrapped handle of her shopping cart, trying to keep up with her racing heart. It was time to make a quick exit. "Thanks again for your help. Maybe I'll see you around the island sometime."

"Good luck with the painting." Derek lifted one hand and let it fall. He had a stack of frames tucked under his other arm.

After checking out and packing the supplies into her Jeep, Lexie wished she hadn't been so skittish around Derek and missed the opportunity to reciprocate his interest in her new hobby. He'd spoken about creativity, and judging by the frames and his knowledge of the Hanapepe street fair, he was probably an artist himself. There she was, thinking about him again. Derek was just another piece of man candy Lexi didn't want to taste, even if he'd been kind and genuine at the store. She shouldn't be mean to him just because she carried a chip on her shoulder the size of the Sears Tower. She could give him the benefit of the doubt. Derek was quite possibly delicious on the inside, too.

Then again, so was the authentic Hawaiian shaved ice Lexi was going to pick up at Hee Fat General Store. Yes, ice covered in sugar sitting on top of a mountain of thick ice cream would definitely do the trick to keep Lexi's mind from wandering into dangerous territory.

Keep reading *Hawaiian Masquerade* and find out more about the Burke Billionaire Romance series at www.rachellechristensen.com

Acknowledgements

I'd like to thank Christina Dymock and Gelato Publishing for believing in my writing and inviting me to join the Destination Billionaire Romance line. I've enjoyed writing these sweet contemporary romances and getting to know so many other fabulous authors.

Thanks to my husband Steve for planning the trip to Nashville so that we could research for this book. Tennessee is a beautiful state and I hope to be able to visit again soon. I'm grateful to my five beautiful children who keep me grounded and inspire me daily. A special thanks to my parents for their encouragement, support, and for being spectacular grandparents!

This book wouldn't have come together without the help of the great team of people who worked on the cover, typesetting, editing, and beta reading. Thank you for your expertise.

And to you, the reader: Thank you for taking time to read my book. I know that there are so many to choose from, and

I'm grateful that you were able to get to know the characters who feel like my friends now.

I'm especially grateful to God for blessing me in so many ways and encouraging me to see His hand in my life daily.

Rachelle J. Christensen

Photo by Erin Summerill

About the Author

Rachelle is a mother of five who writes mystery /suspense, nonfiction, and women's fiction. She solves the case of the missing shoe on a daily basis. She enjoys raising chickens and laughing with her husband. She graduated cum laude from Utah State University with a degree in psychology and a minor in music.

RACHELLE J. CHRISTENSEN

Rachelle is the award-winning author of twenty books, including *The Soldier's Bride (a Kindle Scout Selection)*, *Diamond Rings Are Deadly Things*, *Hawaiian Masquerade*, and *Christmas Kisses: An Echo Ridge Anthology*. Her novella, "Silver Cascade Secrets," was included in the Rone Award–winning *Timeless Romance Anthology, Fall Collection*.

Join Rachelle's VIP mailing list to learn more about upcoming books and get your free book at www.rachellechristensen.com.

Your Free Book is Waiting

FROM AWARD-WINNING AND BESTSELLING AUTHOR
Rachelle J. Christensen

Take one park in autumn, mix in a handsome stranger, a daring heroine, murder, chocolate peanut butter brownies, mystery, and a few kisses and you'll see why *Silver Cascade Secrets* has everything you need to satisfy your cravings for a good read.

amazon kindle nook kobo iBooks

"Great writing, a sweet romance, and an intriguing mystery all rolled into a single story."
--Heather B. Moore, *USA Today* Bestselling Author